Resounding praise for
the incomparable western fiction of
New York Times bestselling Grand Master

ELMORE LEONARD

★

"Leonard began his career telling western stories. He knows his way onto a horse and out of a gun fight as well as he knows the special King's English spoken by his patented, not-so-lovable urban lowlifes."

Milwaukee Journal Sentinel

"In cowboy writing, Leonard belongs in the same A-list shelf as Louis L'Amour, Owen Wister, and Zane Grey."

New York Daily News

"Leonard wrote westerns, very good westerns . . . the way he imagined Hemingway, his mentor, might write westerns."

Baton Rouge Sunday Advocate

"A master . . . Etching a harsh, haunting landscape with razor-sharp prose, Leonard shows in [his] brilliant stories why he has become the American poet laureate of the desperate and the bold . . . In stories that burn with passion, treachery, and heroism, the frontier comes vividly, magnificently to life."

Tulsa World

"[Leonard's stories] transcend the genre to work as well as any serious fiction of the era—or any era."

Chicago Tribune

Books by Elmore Leonard

Trail of the Apache and Other Stories
Three-Ten to Yuma and Other Stories
Blood Money and Other Stories
Moment of Vengeance and Other Stories
The Complete Western Stories of Elmore Leonard
Mr. Paradise
When the Women Come Out to Dance
Tishomingo Blues
Pagan Babies
Be Cool
The Tonto Woman & Other Western Stories
Cuba Libre
Out of Sight
Riding the Rap
Pronto
Rum Punch
Maximum Bob
Get Shorty
Killshot
Freaky Deaky
Touch
Bandits
Glitz
LaBrava
Stick
Cat Chaser
Split Images
City Primeval
Gold Coast
Gunsights
The Switch
The Hunted
Unknown Man No. 89
Swag
Fifty-two Pickup
Mr. Majestyk
Forty Lashes Less One
Valdez Is Coming
The Moonshine War
The Big Bounce
Hombre
Last Stand at Saber River
Escape from Five Shadows
The Law at Randado
The Bounty Hunters

ELMORE
LEONARD

Trail of the Apache

and other stories

HARPER

An Imprint of HarperCollins*Publishers*

This book is a work of fiction. The characters, incidents, and dialogue are drawn from the author's imagination and are not to be construed as real. Any resemblance to actual events, locales or persons, living or dead, is entirely coincidental.

HARPER

An Imprint of HarperCollins*Publishers*
10 East 53rd Street
New York, New York 10022-5299

Map designed by Jane S. Kim
Collection editor, Gregg Sutter
ISBN: 978-0-06-112165-4
ISBN-10: 0-06-112165-7

First Harper paperback printing: February 2007

The stories contained in this volume appeared in *The Complete Western Stories of Elmore Leonard*, published in December 2004 by William Morrow, an imprint of HarperCollins Publishers.

Printed in the United States of America

Visit Harper paperbacks on the World Wide Web at www.harpercollins.com

10 9 8 7 6 5 4 3 2 1

☆ Contents ☆

ARIZONA TERRITORY 1880s
to WHIPPLE BARRACKS
Fort Apache
Fort McDowell
Superstition Mountains
PHOENIX
Inspiration
Apache Junction
San Carlos
San Carlos Apache Indian Reservation
Globe
Hatch & Hodges Central Mail Section
Gila Mountains
Gila Ford
Gila River
Rindo's Station
White Tanks
Pinaleno Mountains
Fort Thomas
Casa Grande
Florence
to YUMA
Fort Grant
to LAS CRUCES, NEW MEXICO
N
W
E
S
San Pedro River
Fort Bowie
Willcox
Dos Cabezas Mountains
Tucson
Dos Cabezas
Dragoon Mountains
Benson
Canyon Diablo
Contention
Tombstone
Arivaca
Sweetmary
Sasabe
Fort Huachuca
Bisbee
Nogales
Douglas

1

Trail of the Apache

UNDER THE THATCHED roof ramada that ran the length of the agency office, Travisin slouched in a canvas-backed chair, his boots propped against one of the support posts. His gaze took in the sun-beaten, gray adobe buildings, all one-story structures, that rimmed the vacant quadrangle. It was a glaring, depressing scene of sun on rock, without a single shade tree or graceful feature to redeem the squat ugliness. There was not a living soul in sight. Earlier that morning, his White Mountain Apache charges had received their two-weeks' supply of beef and flour. By now they were milling about the cook fires in front of their wickiups, eating up a two-weeks' ration in two days. Most of the Indians had built their wickiups three miles farther up the Gila, where the flat, dry land began to buckle into rock-strewn hills. There the thin, sparse Gila cottonwoods grew taller and closer together and the mesquite and prickly pear thicker. And there was the small game that sustained them when their government rations were consumed.

At the agency, Travisin lived alone. By actual count there were forty-two Coyotero Apache scouts along with the interpreter, Barney Fry, and his wife, a Tonto woman, but as the officers at Fort Thomas looked at it, he was living alone. There is no question that to most young Eastern gentlemen on frontier station, such an alien means of existence would have meant nothing more than a very slow way to die, with boredom reading the services. But, of course, they were not Travisin.

* * *

FROM WHIPPLE BARRACKS, through San Carlos and on down to Fort Huachuca, it went without argument that Eric Travisin was the best Apache campaigner in Arizona Territory. There was a time, of course, when this belief was not shared by all and the question would pop up often, along the trail, in the barracks at Fort Thomas, or in a Globe barroom. Barney Fry's name would always come up then—though most discounted him for his one-quarter Apache blood. But that was a time in the past when Eric Travisin was still new; before the sweltering sand-rock Apache country had burned and gouged his features, leaving his gaunt face deep-chiseled and expressionless. That was while he was learning that it took an Apache to catch an Apache. So, for all practical purposes, he became one. Barney Fry taught him everything he knew about the Apache; then he began teaching Fry. He relied on no one entirely, not even Fry. He followed his own judgment, a judgment that his fellow officers looked upon as pure animal instinct. And perhaps they were right. But Travisin understood the steps necessary to survival in an enemy element. They weren't included in Cook's "Cavalry Tactics": you learned them the hard way, and your being alive testified that you had learned well. They said Travisin was more of an Apache than the Apaches themselves. They said he was cold-blooded, sometimes cruel. And they were uneasy in his presence; he had discarded his cotillion demeanor the first year at Fort Thomas, and in its place was the quiet, pulsing fury of an Apache war dance.

This was easy enough for the inquisitive to understand. But there was another side to Eric Travisin.

For three years he had been acting as agent at the Camp Gila subagency, charged with the health and welfare of over two hundred White Mountain Apaches. And in three years he had transformed nomadic hostiles into peaceful agriculturalists. He was a dismounted cavalry officer who sometimes laid it on with the flat of his saber, but he was completely honest. He understood them and took their side, and they respected him for it. It was better than San Carlos.

That's why the conversation at the officers' mess at Fort Thomas, thirty miles southwest, so often dwelled on him: he was a good Samaritan with a Spencer in his hand. They just didn't understand him. They didn't realize that actually he was following the line of least resistance. He was accepting the situation as it was and doing the best job with the means at hand. To Travisin it was that simple; and fortunately he enjoyed it, both the fighting and the pacifying. The fact that it made him a better cavalryman never entered his mind. He had forgotten about promotions. By this time he was too much a part of the savage everyday existence of Apache country. He looked at the harsh, rugged surroundings and liked what he saw.

He shuffled his feet up and down the porch pole and sank deeper into his camp chair. Suddenly in his breast he felt the tenseness. His ears seemed to tingle and strain against an unnatural stillness, and immediately every muscle tightened. But as quickly as the strange feeling came over him, he relaxed.

He moved his head no more than two inches, and from the corner of his eye saw the Apache crouched on hands and knees at the corner of the ramada. The Indian crept like an animal across the porch, slowly and with his back arched. A pistol and a knife were at his waist, but he carried no weapon in his hands. Travisin moved his right hand across his stomach and eased open the holster flap. Now his arms were folded across his chest, with his right hand gripping the holstered pistol. He waited until the Apache was less than six feet away before he wheeled from his chair and pushed the long-barreled revolving pistol into the astonished Apache's face.

Travisin grinned at the Apache and holstered the handgun. "Maybe someday you'll do it."

The Indian grunted angrily. With victory almost in his grasp he had failed again. Gatito, sergeant of Travisin's Apache scouts, was an old man, the best tracker in the Army, and it cut his pride deeply that he was never able to win their wager. Between the two men was an unusual bet of almost two years' standing. If at any time, while not officially occupied, the scout was able to steal up to the officer and place his knife at Travisin's back, a bottle of whiskey was his. For such a prize the Indian would gladly crawl through anything. He tried constantly, using every trick he knew, but the officer was always ready. The result was a grumbling, thirsty Indian, but an officer whose senses were razor-sharp. Travisin even practiced staying alive.

Gatito gave the report of the morning patrol and then added, almost as an afterthought, "Chiricahua come. Two miles away."

Travisin wheeled from the office doorway. "Where?"

Gatito spoke impassively. "Chiricahua come. He come with troop from Fort."

Travisin considered the Apache's words in silence, squinting through the afternoon glare toward the wooden bridge across the Gila that was the end of the trail from Thomas. They would come from that direction. "Go get Fry immediately. And turn out your boys."

☆

Chapter Two

Second Lieutenant William de Both, West Point's newest contribution to the "Dandy 5th," had the distinct feeling that he was entering a hostile camp as he led H troop across the wooden bridge and approached Camp Gila. As he drew nearer to the agency office, the figures in front of it appeared no friendlier. Good God, were they all Indians? After guarding the sixteen hostiles the thirty miles from

Fort Thomas, Lieutenant de Both had had enough of Indians for a long time. Even with the H troopers riding four sides, he couldn't help glancing nervously back to the sixteen hostiles and expecting trouble to break out at any moment. After thirty miles of this, he was hardly prepared to face the gaunt, raw-boned Travisin and his sinister-looking band of Apache scouts.

His fellow officers back at Fort Thomas had eagerly informed de Both of the character of the formidable Captain Travisin. In fact, they painted a picture of him with bold, harsh strokes, watching the young lieutenant's face intently to enjoy the mixed emotions that showed so obviously. But even with the exaggerated tales of the officers' mess, de Both could not help learning that this unusual Indian agent was still the best army officer on the frontier. Three months out of the Point, he was only too eager to serve under the best.

Leading his troop across the square, he scanned the ragged line of men in front of the office and on the ramada. All were armed, and all stared at the approaching column as if it were bringing cholera instead of sixteen unarmed Indians. He halted the column and dismounted in front of the tall, thin man in the center. The lieutenant inspected the man's faded blue chambray shirt and gray trousers, and unconsciously adjusted his own blue jacket.

"My man, would you kindly inform the captain that Lieutenant de Both is reporting? I shall present my orders to him." The lieutenant was brushing trail dust from his sleeve as he spoke.

Travisin stood with hands on hips looking at de Both. He shook his head faintly, without speaking, and began to twist one end of his dragoon mustache. Then he nodded to the foremost of the Chiricahuas and turned to Barney Fry.

"Barney, that's Pillo, isn't it?"

"Ain't nobody else," the scout said matter-of-factly. "And the skinny buck on the paint is Asesino, his son-in-law."

Travisin turned his attention to the bewildered lieutenant. "Well, mister, ordinarily I'd play games with you for a while, but under the circumstances, when you bring along company like that, we'd better get down to the business at hand without the monkeyshines. Fry, take care of our guests. Lieutenant, you come with me." He turned abruptly and entered the office.

Inside, de Both pulled out a folded sheet of paper and handed it to Travisin. The captain sat back, propped his boots on the desk and read the orders slowly. When he was through, he shook his head and silently cursed the stupidity of men trying to control a powder-keg situation two thousand miles from the likely explosion. He read the orders again to be certain that the content was as illogical as it seemed.

HEADQUARTERS, DEPARTMENT OF ARIZONA
IN THE FIELD, FORT THOMAS, ARIZONA
August 30, 1880
E. M. Travisin. Capt. 5th Cav. Reg.
Camp Gila Subagency
Camp Gila, Arizona

You are hereby directed, by order of the Department of the Interior, Bureau of Indian Affairs, to place Pillo and the remnants of his band (numbering fifteen) on the Camp Gila White Mountain reservation. The Bureau compliments you on the remarkable job you are doing and has confidence that the sixteen hostile Chiricahuas, placed in your charge, will profit by the example of their White Mountain brothers and become peaceful farmers.

The bearer, Second Lieutenant William de Both, is, as of this writing, assigned to Camp Gila as second in command. Take him under your wing, Eric; he's young, but I think he will make a good officer.

EMON COLLIER
BRIGADIER GENERAL COMMANDING

He looked up at the lieutenant, who was gazing about the bare room, taking in the table, the rolltop desk along the back wall, the rifle rack and three straight chairs. De Both looked no more than twenty-one or -two, pink-cheeked, neat, every inch a West Point gentleman. But already, after only three months on the frontier, his face was beginning to lose that expression of anticipated adventure, the young officer's dream of winning fame and promotion in the field. The thirty miles from Fort Thomas alone presented the field as something he had not bargained for. To Travisin, it wasn't a new story. He'd had younger officers serve under him before, and it always started the same way, ". . . take him under your wing . . . teach him about the Apache." It was always the old campaigner teaching the recruit what it was all about.

To Eric Travisin, at twenty-eight, only seven years out of the Point, it was bound to be amusing. The cavalry mustache made him look older, but that wasn't it. Travisin had been a veteran his first year. It was something that he'd had even before he came West. It was that something that made him stand out in any group of men. It was the strange instinct that made him wheel and draw his handgun when Gatito stole up behind him. It was a combination of many things, but not one of them did Travisin himself understand, even though they made him the youngest captain in Arizona because of it.

And now another one to watch him and not understand. He wondered how long de Both would last.

He said, "Lieutenant, do you know why you've been sent here?"

"No, sir." De Both brought himself to attention. "I do not question my orders."

Travisin was faintly amused. "I'm sure you don't, Lieutenant. I was referring to any rumors you might have heard. . . . And relax."

De Both remained at attention. "I don't make it a practice to repeat idle rumors that have no basis in fact."

Travisin felt his temper rise, but suppressed it from long practice. It wasn't the way to get things done. He circled the desk and drew a chair up behind de Both. "Here, rest your legs." He placed a firm hand on the lieutenant's shoulder and half forced him into the chair. "Mister, you and I are going to spend a lot of time together. We'll be either in this room or out on the desert with nothing to think about except what's in front of us. Conversation gets pretty thin after a while, and you might even make up things just to hear yourself talk. You're the only other Regular Army man here, so you can see it isn't going to be a parade-grounds routine. I've been here for three years now, counting White Mountain Indians and making patrols. Sometimes things get a bit hot; otherwise you just sit around and watch the desert. I probably don't look like much of an officer to you. That doesn't matter. You can keep up the spit and polish if you want, but I'd advise you to relax and play the game without keeping the rule book open all the time. . . . Now, would you mind telling me what in hell the rumors are at Thomas?"

★ ★ ★

DE BOTH WAS surprised, and disturbed. He fidgeted in his chair, trying to feel official. "Well, sir, under the circumstances . . . Of course, as I said, there is no basis for its authenticity, but the word is that Crook is being transferred back to the Department to lead an expedition to the border. They say that he will probably ask for you. So I am being assigned here to replace you when the time comes. This is, of course, only gossip that is circulating about."

"Do you believe it?"

"Sir, I don't even think about it."

Travisin said, "You mean you don't want to think about it. Sitting by yourself at a Godforsaken Indian agency with almost two hundred and fifty White Mountains living across the street. Not to mention the scouts." He paused and smiled at de Both. "I don't know, Lieutenant, you might even like it after a while."

"I accept my orders, Captain. My desires have nothing to do with my orders."

But Travisin was not listening. Long strides took

him to the doorway and he leaned out with a hand against the door frame on each side.

"Fryyyyyyyyyyy! Hey, Fryyyy!"

★ ★ ★

THE MEN OF H troop looked over to the office as they prepared to mount. Barney Fry left the sergeant and strode toward the agency office. "Come in here, Barney."

The clatter of trotting horses beat across the quadrangle as Fry stepped up on the porch and entered the office. His short strides were slightly pigeon-toed and he held his head tilted down as if he were self-conscious of his appearance. He looked to be in his early twenties, but, like Travisin, his face was a hard, bronzed mask, matured beyond his age. When he took off his gray widebrimmed hat, thick, black hair clung close to his scalp, smeared with oily perspiration.

"What do you think, Barney?"

Fry leaned against the edge of the desk. "I think probably the same thing you do. Those 'Paches aren't goin' to stay long at Gila even if we'd give them all the beef critters in Arizona. You notice there wasn't any women in the band?"

"Yes, I noticed," Travisin answered. "They'll never learn, will they?" He looked at de Both. "You see, Lieutenant, the Bureau thinks that if they separate them from their families for a while, the hostiles will become good little Indians and make plows out of their Spencers and grow corn to eat instead of drink. What would you do if some benevolent race snatched your women and children from you and sent you to a barren rock pile over a hundred miles away? And do you know why? For something you'd been doing for the past three hundred years. For that simple but enigmatic something that makes you an Apache and not a Navajo. For that quirk of fate that makes you a tiger instead of a Persian cat. Mister, I've got over two hundred White Mountains here raising crops and eating government beef. I can assure you that they're not doing it by nature! And now they sent sixteen Chiricahuas! Sixteen men with the smell of gunpowder still strong in their nostrils and blood lust in their eyes." Travisin shook his head wearily. "And they send them here without their women."

De Both cleared his throat before speaking. "Well, frankly, Captain, I don't see what the problem is. Obviously, these hostiles have done wrong. The natural consequence would be a punishment of some sort. Why pamper them? They're not little children."

"No, they're not little children. They're Apaches," Travisin reflected. "You know, I used to know an Indian up near Fort Apache by the name of Skimitozin. He was an Arivaipa. One day he was sitting in the hut of a white friend of his, a miner, and they were eating supper together. Then, for no reason at all, Skimitozin drew his handgun and shot his friend through the head. Before they hung him he said he did it to show his Arivaipa people that they should never get too friendly with the *blancos*. The Apache has never gotten a real break from the whites. So Skimitozin wanted to make sure that his people never got to the point of expecting one, and relaxing. Mister, I'm here to kill Indians and keep Indians alive. It's a paradox—no question about that—but I gave up rationalizing a long time ago. Most Apaches have always lived a life of violence. I'm not here primarily to convert them; but by the same token I have to be fair—when they are fair to me."

De Both raised an objection. "I see nothing wrong with our treatment of the Indians. As a matter of fact, I think we've gone out of our way to treat them decently." He recited the words as if he were reading from an official text.

Fry broke in. "Go up to San Carlos and spend a week or two," he said. "Especially when the government beef contractors come around with their adjusted scales and each cow with a couple of barrels of Gila water in her. Watch how the 'Pache women try to cut each other up for a bloated cow belly." Fry spoke slowly, without excitement.

Travisin said to the lieutenant, "Fry's not talking

about one or two incidents. He's talking about history. You were with Pillo all the way up from Thomas. Did you see his eyes? If you did, you saw the whole story."

☆

Chapter Three

The early afternoon sun blazed heavily against the adobe houses and vacant quadrangle. The air was still, still and oppressive, and seemed to be thickened by the fierce, withering rays of the Arizona sun. To the east, the purplish blur of the Pinals showed hazily through the glare.

Travisin leaned loosely against a support post under the brush ramada. His gray cotton shirt was black with sweat in places, but he seemed unmindful of the heat. His sun-darkened face was impassive, as if asleep, but his eyes were only half closed in the shadow of his hat brim, squinting against the glare in the direction from which Fry would return.

Earlier that morning, the scout and six of his Coyoteros had traveled upriver to inspect the tracts selected by Pillo and his band. The hostiles had erected their wickiups without a murmur of complaint and seemed to have fallen into the alien routines of reservation life without any trouble; but it was their silence, their impassive acceptance of this new life that bothered Travisin. For the two weeks the hostiles had been at Camp Gila, Travisin's scouts had been on the alert every minute of the day. But nothing had happened. When Fry returned, he would know more.

De Both appeared in the office door behind him. "Not back yet?"

"No. He might have stopped to chin with some of the White Mountain people. He's got a few friends there," Travisin said. "Barney's got a little Apache blood in him, you know."

De Both was openly surprised. "He has? I didn't know that!" He thought of the countless times he had voiced his contempt for the Apaches in front of Fry. He felt uncomfortable and a little embarrassed now, though Fry had never once seemed to take it as a personal affront. Travisin read the discomfort on his face. There was no sense in making it more difficult.

* * *

"His mother was a half-breed," Travisin explained. "She married a miner and followed him all over the Territory while he dug holes in the ground. Barney was born somewhere up in the Tonto country on one of his dad's claims. When he was about eight or nine his ma and dad were killed by some Tontos and he was carried off and brought up in the tribe. That's where he got his nose for scouting.

It's not just in his blood like some people think; he learned it, and he learned it from the best in the business. Then, when he was about fifteen, he came back to the world of the whites. About that time there was a campaign operating out of Fort Apache against the Tontos. One day a patrol came across the rancheria where Barney lived and took him back to Fort Apache. All the warriors were out and only the women and children were around. He remembered enough about the white man's life to want to go back to the Indians, but he knew too much about the Apache's life for the Army to let him go; so he's been a guide since that day. He was at Fort Thomas when I arrived there seven years ago, and he's been with me ever since I've been here at Gila."

De Both was deep in thought. "But can you trust him?" he asked. "After living with the Apaches for so long."

"Can you trust the rest of the scouts? Can you trust those rocks and mesquite clumps out yonder?" Travisin looked hard into the lieutenant's eyes. "Mister, you watch the rocks, the trees, the men around you. You watch until your eyes ache, and then you keep on watching. Because you'll always have that feeling that the minute you let down, you're done for. And if you don't have that feeling, you're in the wrong business."

A little past four, Fry and his scouts rode in. He

threw off and ran toward the agency office. Travisin met him in the doorway. "They scoot, Barney?"

★ ★ ★

FRY PAUSED TO catch his breath and wiped the sweat from his face with a grimy, brown hand.

"It might be worse than that. When we got there this morning only a few of Pillo's band were around. I questioned them, but they kept trying to change the subject and get us out of there. I thought they were actin' strange, talkin' more than usual, and then it dawned on me. Gatito had spotted it right away. They'd been drinkin' tizwin. You know you got to drink a whoppin' lot of that stuff to really get drunk. I figure these boys ain't had much yet, cuz they were still too quiet. But the others were probably off at the source of supply so we rode out and tried to cut their sign. We tried every likely spot in the neighborhood until after noon, and we still couldn't find a trace of them."

Travisin considered the situation silently for a moment. "They've probably been at it since they got here. Taking their time to pick a spot we wouldn't find right away. No wonder they've been so quiet." Travisin had much to think about, for a drunken Apache will do strange things. Bloody things. He asked the scout, "What does Gatito think?"

Fry hesitated, and then said, "I don't like the way he was lickin' his lips while we were on the hunt."

Fry did not have to say more. Travisin knew him well enough to know that the scout felt Gatito could bear some extra attention. To de Both, watching the scene, it was a new experience. The captain and the quarter-breed scout talking like brothers. Saying more with eyes and gestures than with words. He looked from one to the other intently, then for the first time noticed the young Apache standing next to Travisin. A moment ago he had not been there. But there had not been a sound or a footstep!

The young brave spoke swiftly in the Apache tongue for almost a minute and then disappeared around the corner of the office. De Both could still see vividly the red calico cloth around thick, black hair, and his almost feminine features.

Fry and Travisin began to talk again, but de Both interrupted.

"What in the name of heaven was that?"

Travisin grinned at the young officer's astonishment. "I thought you knew Peaches. Forgot he hadn't been around for a while."

"Peaches!"

Travisin said, "Let's go inside."

They gathered around his table, lighted cigarettes, and Travisin went on. "I'd just as soon you didn't speak his name aloud around here. You see, that young, gentle-looking Apache has one of the toughest jobs on the reservation. He's an agency spy. Only Fry and I, and now you, know what he is. Not even any of the scouts know. The Indians suspect that someone on their side is reporting to me, but they have no idea who it is. He's got a dangerous job, but it's necessary. If trouble ever breaks out, we have to be able to nip it in the bud. Peaches is the only way for us to determine where the bud is."

"May I ask what he told you just now?"

Travisin drew hard on his cigarette before replying. "He said that he knew much, but he would be back sometime before sunup tomorrow to tell what he knew. He made one last point very emphatic. He said, 'Watch Gatito!' "

★ ★ ★

A REAR ROOM of the agency office adobe served as sleeping quarters for both of the officers. Their cots were against opposite walls, lockers at the feet, and two large pine-board wardrobes, holding uniforms and personal gear, were flush with the wall running along the heads of their bunks.

A full moon pointed its light through the window frame over de Both's bed, carpeted the plank flooring with a delicate sheen, and reached as far as the gleaming upper portion of Travisin's body, motionless on the cot. One arm was beneath the gray blanket that reached just above his waist, the other was folded across his bare chest.

A floorboard creaked somewhere near. His eyes

opened at once and closed just as suddenly. Beneath the blanket his hand groped near his thigh and quietly covered the grip of his pistol. He opened his eyes slightly and glanced across the room. De Both was dead asleep. The latch on the door leading to the front office rattled faintly, and then hinges creaked as the door began to open. Travisin quietly drew his arm from beneath the blanket and leveled the pistol at the doorway. His thumb closed on the hammer and drew it back, and the click of the cocking action was a sharp, metallic sound. The opening-door motion stopped.

"Nantan, do not shoot." The words were just above a whisper.

Travisin threw the blanket from his legs, swung them to the floor and moved to the doorway without a sound. Peaches backed into the office as he approached.

"Chiricahua leave."

"How long?"

"They go maybe five mile now. Gatito go with them."

Travisin stepped back to the doorway and slammed the butt of his pistol against the wooden door. "Hey, mister, roll out!" De Both sat bolt upright. "Be ready to ride in a few minutes," Travisin said, and ran out of the office toward Barney Fry's adobe across the quadrangle.

In less than twenty minutes, thirteen riders

streaked out of the quadrangle westward. Behind them, orange light was just beginning to show above the irregular outline of the Pinals. The morning was cool, but still, and the stillness held the promise of the blistering heat of the day to come.

The sun was only a little higher when Travisin and his scouts rode up to four wickiups along the bank of the Gila. Travisin halted the detail, but did not dismount. He sat motionless in the saddle, his senses alert to the quiet. He said something in Apache and one of the scouts threw off and cautiously entered the first wickiup. He reappeared in an instant, shaking his head from side to side. In the third hut, the scout remained longer than usual. When he reappeared he was dragging an unconscious Indian by the legs.

Travisin said, "That one of them, Barney?"

Fry swung down from his pony and leaned over the prostrate Indian, saying a few words in Apache to the scout still holding the Indian's legs. "He's a Chiricahua, Captain. Dead drunk. Must have been drinking for at least two days." He nodded his head toward the Apache scout. "Ningun says there's a jug inside with a little tizwin in it."

Travisin pointed to two of the scouts and then swept his arm in the direction of the fourth wickiup. They kicked their ponies to a leaping start, dashed to the hut and gave it a quick inspection. In a minute they were back.

The scouts watched Travisin intently as he studied the situation. They knew what the signs meant. They sat their ponies now with restless anticipation, fingering their carbines, checking ammunition belts, holding in the small, wiry horses that also seemed to be charged with the excitement of the moment—for there is no love lost between the Coyotero and the Chiricahua. Eric Travisin knew as well as any of them what the sign meant: sixteen drunken Apaches screaming through the countryside with blood in their eyes and a bad taste in their mouths. It was something that had to be stopped before the Indians regained their senses. Now they were loco Apaches, bloodthirsty, but a bit careless. By the next day, unless stopped, they would again be cold, patient guerrilla fighters led by the master strategist, Pillo.

★ ★ ★

FROM THE DIRECTION of the agency a scout rode into sight beating his pony to a whirlwind pace. He reined in abruptly and shouted something to Fry through the dust cloud.

"We been sleepin', Captain. He says Gatito made off with a dozen carbines and two hundred rounds of forty-fours. Must have sneaked them out sometime last night."

In Travisin, the excitement of what lay ahead was building up continually. Now it was beginning to break through his calm surface. "We're awake now, Barney. I figure they'll either streak south for the Madres right away, or contact their people up near Apache by dodging through the Basin and then heading east for the reservation. I know if I was going to hide out for a while, I'd sure want my wife along. Let's find out which it is."

☆

Chapter Four

By midmorning Travisin's scouts had followed the tracks of the hostiles to an elevated stretch of pines wedged tightly among bare, rolling hills. They halted a few hundred yards from the wooded area, in the open. Before them the land, dotted with mesquite and catclaw, climbed gradually to the pine plateau; and the sun-glare made shimmering waves, hazy and filmy white, as they looked ahead to the contrasting black of the pines. A shallow arroyo cut its way down from the ridge past where the detail stood, finally ending at the banks of the Gila, twelve miles behind them. On both sides of the crusted edges of the arroyo, the unshod tracks they had been following all morning moved straight ahead.

Ningun, the Apache scout, rode up the arroyo a hundred yards, circled and returned. He mumbled only a few words to Fry, who glanced at the pine ridge again before speaking.

"He says the tracks go all the way up. Ain't no other place they could go."

"Does he think they're still up there?" Travisin asked the question without taking his eyes from the ridge.

"He didn't say, but I know he don't think so." Barney Fry pulled out a tobacco plug and bit off a generous chew, mumbling, "And I don't either." He moved the front of his open vest aside with a thumb and dropped the plug into the pocket of his shirt. "I figure it this way, Captain," he said. "They know who's followin' 'em, and they know we ain't about to get caught in a simple jackpot like that one up yonder without flushin' it out first. So they ain't goin' to waste their time settin' a trap that we won't fall right into."

"Sounds good, Barney, only there's one thing that's been troubling me," Travisin said. "Notice how clean the sign's been all the way? Not once have they tried to throw us off the track—and they've had more than one opportunity to at least make it pretty tough. No Apache, no matter if he's drunker than seven hundred dollars, is going to leave a trail that plain—that is, unless he wants to." He looked at the scout, suggesting a reply with his expression, and added, "Now why do you suppose old Pillo would want us to follow him?"

Fry pushed his hat from his forehead and passed the back of his hand across his mouth. It was plain that the captain's words gave him something to think about, but he had been riding with Travisin too long to show surprise with the officer's uncanny familiarity with what an Apache would do at a given time. He was never absolutely sure himself, but for some unexplainable reason Travisin's judgment was almost always right. And when dealing with an unknown quantity, the Apache, this judgment sometimes seemed to reach a superhuman level.

Fry was quiet, busy putting himself in Pillo's place, but de Both spoke up at once. "I take it you're suggesting that the Indians are not really drunk. But what about that unconscious Indian back at the reservation?" He asked the question as if he were purposely trying to shoot holes in the captain's theory.

"No, Lieutenant. I'm only saying what if," Travisin agreed, with a faint smile. "Could be one way or the other. I just want to impress you that we're not chasing Harvard sophomores across the Boston Common. If you ever come up against a better general than Pillo, you can be sure of one thing—he'll be another Apache."

Though he was sure of Fry's and Ningun's judgment, Travisin sent scouts ahead to flank the pine woods before taking his command through.

In another hour they were over the ridge, in the open, descending noisily over the loose gravel that was strewn down the gradual slope that led to the valley below. On level ground again, they followed the tracks to the north, up the raw, rolling valley, flat and straight from a distance; but as they traveled, the sandrock ground buckled and heaved into shallow crevices and ditches every few hundred feet. The monotony of the bleak scene was interrupted only by the grotesque outlines of giant saguaro and low, thick mesquite clumps.

Even in this comparatively open ground, de Both noticed that Travisin and all of the scouts rode half-tensed in their saddles, their eyes sweeping the area to the front and to both sides, studying every rock or shrub clump large enough to conceal a man. It was a vigilance that he himself was slowly acquiring just from noticing the others. Still he was more than willing to let the scouts do the watching. The damned stifling heat and the dazzling glare were enough for a white man to worry about. He mopped his face continually, and every once in a while pulled the white bandanna around his throat up over his nose and mouth. But that caused the heat to be even more smothering. He could feel the Apache scouts laughing at him. How could they remain so damned cool-looking in this heat! With every step of the horses, the dust rose around him and seemed to cling to his lungs until he would cough and cover his nose again with the kerchief. Ahead, but slightly to the east, he studied the jagged, blue outline of a mountain range. The Sierra Apaches. The purplish blue of the mountains and the soft blue of the cloudless sky were the only pleasant tones to redeem the ragged, wild look of the valley.

He pressed his heels into his horse's flanks and rode up abreast of Travisin. The climate and the unyielding country were grinding de Both's nerves raw; he wanted to scream at somebody, anybody.

"I sincerely hope you know where you're going, Captain."

★ ★ ★

TRAVISIN IGNORED the sarcasm. "You'll feel better after we camp this evening. First day's always the toughest." He was silent for a few minutes, his head swinging in an arc studying the signs that did not even exist to de Both, and then he added, "Those mountains up ahead are the Sierra Apaches. Lot farther than they look. Before we pass them we're going to camp at a rancher's place. His name's Solomon, a really fine old gentleman. I think you'll like him, Bill." It was the first time Travisin had used de Both's first name. The lieutenant looked at him strangely.

★ ★ ★

IT WAS CLOSE to six o'clock when they reached the road leading to Solomon's place. The road cut an arc through the brush flat and then passed through a grove of cottonwoods. From where they stood, they could see the roof of the ranch house through the clearing in the trees made by the road. The house stood a few hundred yards the other side of the cottonwoods, and just to the right of it a few acres of pines edged toward the house from the foothills of the Sierra Apaches towering to the east. Fry pointed to the wide path of trampled brush a hundred feet to the left of the road they were following.

"There's one I wouldn't care to try to figure out. Why didn't they take the road?"

Travisin was watching Ningun circle the cottonwoods and head back. "They're making it a bit *too* easy now," he replied idly.

Ningun made his report to Fry and pointed above the cottonwoods in the direction of the pines. A faint wisp of dark smoke curled skyward in a thin line. Against the glare it was hardly noticeable.

"Know what that means?" Travisin asked. He looked at no one in particular.

Fry answered, "I got an idea."

They dismounted in the cottonwoods and approached the clearing on foot. The ranch house, barn and corral behind it seemed deserted.

Travisin said, "Go take a look, Barney." Fry beckoned to four of the Apache scouts and they followed him into the clearing. They walked across the open space toward the house slowly, all abreast.

They made no attempt to conceal themselves by crouching or hunching their shoulders—a natural instinct, but futile precaution with no cover in sight. They walked perfectly erect with their carbines out in front. Suddenly they all stopped and one of the scouts dropped to his hands and knees and put his ear to the earth. He arose slowly, and the others back at the cottonwoods saw them watching the pines more closely as they approached the house. Fry walked up to the log wall next to the front door and placed his ear to it. He made a motion with his right hand and three of the scouts disappeared around the corner of the house. Without hesitating, Fry approached the front door, kicked it open and darted into the dimness of the interior, the fourth Apache scout behind him. In a few moments, Fry reappeared in the doorway and waved to the rest in the cottonwoods.

He was still in the doorway when Travisin brought the others up. "Just the missus is inside" was all he said.

Travisin, with de Both behind him, walked past the scout into the dimly lit ranch house. The room was a shambles, every piece of furniture and china broken. But what checked their gaze was Mrs. Solomon lying in the middle of the floor. Her clothes had been almost entirely ripped from her body and the flesh showing was gouged and slashed with knife wounds. Her scalp had been torn from her head.

De Both stared at the dead woman with a frozen gaze. Then the revulsion of it overcame him and he half turned to escape into the fresh air outside. He checked himself, thinking then of Travisin, and turned back to the room. The captain and the scout studied the scene stoically; but beneath their impassive eyes, almost any kind of emotion could be present. He tried to show the same calm. A cavalry officer should be used to the sight of death. But this was a form of death de Both had not counted on. He wheeled abruptly and left the room.

The next step was the pines. Travisin ordered the horses put in the corral. In case of a fight, they would be better off afoot; though he was sure that Pillo was hours away by now. They threaded through the nearer, sparsely growing pines that gradually grew taller and heavier as they advanced up the almost unnoticeable grade. Soon the pines entwined with junipers and thick clumps of brush so that they could see no more than fifty feet ahead into the dimness. They were far enough into the thicket so that they could no longer see the wisp of smoke, but now a strange odor took its place. The Coyotero scouts sniffed the air and looked at Travisin.

* * *

FRY SAID, "I'LL send some of 'em ahead," and without waiting for a reply called an order to Ningun in the Apache tongue. As five of the scouts went on ahead, he said, "Let 'em do a little work for their pay," and propped his carbine against a pine. He eased his back against the same tree and looked at Travisin.

"You know, that's a funny thing back there at the cabin," Fry said, pointing his thumb over his shoulder. "That's only the second time in my life that I ever knew of a 'Pache scalpin' anybody."

"I was thinking about that myself," Travisin answered. "Then I remembered hearing once that Pillo was one of the few Apaches with Quana Parker at Adobe Walls six years ago. Don't know how Apaches got tied up with Commanches, but some Commanche dog soldier might have taught him the trick."

"Well," Fry reflected, picking up his carbine, "that's about the only trick a 'Pache might be taught."

Ningun appeared briefly through the trees ahead and waved his arm. They walked out to where he stood. Fry and Travisin listened to Ningun speak and then looked past his drooping shoulders to where he pointed. The nauseating odor was almost unbearable here. De Both tried to hold his breath as he followed the others into a small clearing. In front of him, Travisin and the scout moved apart as they reached the open ground and de Both was struck with a scene he was to remember to his dying day. He stared wide-eyed, swallowing repeatedly, until he could no longer control the saliva rising in his throat, and he turned off the path to be sick.

Fry scraped a boot along the crumbly earth and kicked sand onto the smoldering fire. The smoke rose heavy and thick for a few seconds, obscuring the grotesque form that hung motionless over the center of the small fire; and then it died out completely, revealing the half-burned body of Solomon suspended head-down from the arc of three thin juniper poles that had been stuck into the ground a few feet apart and lashed together at the tops. The old man's head hung only three feet above the smothered ashes of the fire. His head and upper portion of his body were burned beyond recognition, the black rawness creeping from this portion of his body upward to where his hands were tied tightly to his thighs; there the blackness changed to livid red blisters. All of his clothing had been burned away, but his boots still clung to his legs, squeezed to his ankles where the rawhide thongs wound about them and reached above to the arch of junipers. He was dead. But death had come slowly.

"The poor old man." The words were simple, but Travisin's voice cracked just faintly to tell more. "The poor, poor old man."

Fry looked around the clearing slowly, thinking, and then he said, "Bet he screamed for a bullet. Bet he screamed until his throat burst, and all the time they'd just be dancin' around jabbin' him with their knives and laughin'." Fry stopped and looked at the captain.

Travisin stared at old Solomon without blinking, his jaw muscles tightening and relaxing, his teeth grinding against one another. Only once in a while did Fry see him as the young man with feelings. It was a strange sight, the man fighting the boy; but always the man would win and he would go on as relentlessly as before, but with an added ruthlessness that had been sharpened by the emotional surge. Travisin never dealt in half measures. He felt sorrow for the old man cut to the bottom of his stomach, and he swore to himself a revenge, silently, though the fury of it pounded in his head.

☆

Chapter Five

They camped at Solomon's cabin that night, after burying the man and woman, and were up before dawn, in the saddle again on the trail of Pillo. They rode more anxiously now. Caution was still there, for that was instinct with Travisin and the scouts, but every man in the small company could feel an added eagerness, a gnawing urge to hound Pillo's spoor to the end and bring about a violent revenge.

De Both sensed it in himself and saw it easily in the way the Apache scouts clutched their carbines and fingered the triggers almost nervously. He felt the tightness rise in him and felt as if he must shriek to be relieved of the tension. Then he knew that it was the quickness of action mounting within him, that charge placed in a man's breast when he has to go on to kill or be killed. He watched Travisin for a sign to follow, a way in which to react; but as before he saw only the impassive, sun-scarred mask, the almost indolent look of half-closed eyes searching the surroundings for an unfamiliar sign.

By early afternoon, the thrill of the chase was draining from Second Lieutenant William de Both. His legs ached from the long hours in the saddle, and he gazed ahead, welcoming the green valley stretching as far as the eye could see, twisting among rocky hills, looking thick and cool. Over the next rise, they forded the Salt River, shallow and motionless, just west of Cherry Creek, and continued toward the wild, rugged rock and greenery in the distance. De Both heard Fry mention that it was the southern edges of the Tonto Basin, but the name meant little to him.

Toward sundown they were well into the wildness of the Basin. For de Both, the promise of a shady relief had turned into an even more tortuous ride. Through thick, stabbing chapparal and over steep, craggy mounds of rock they made their way.

The trees were there, but they offered no solace; they only urged a stronger caution. The sun was falling fast when Travisin stopped the group on the shoulder of a grassy ridge. Below them the ground fell gradually to the west, green and smooth, extending for a mile to a tangle of trees and brush that began to climb another low hill. Behind it, three or four miles in the distance, the facing sun painted a last, brilliant yellow streak across the jagged top of a mountain.

★ ★ ★

NINGUN JUMPED DOWN from his pony as the others dismounted, and stared across the grass valley for a full minute or more. Then he spoke in English, pointing to the light-streaked mountain of rock. "There you find Pillo."

Fry conversed with him in Apache for a while, shooting an occasional question at one of the other scouts, and then said to Travisin, "They all agree that's most likely where Pillo is. One of 'em says Pillo used to have a rancheria up there. Pro'bly a favorite spot of his." The scout sat down in the grass and reached for his tobacco chew.

Travisin squatted next to him, Indian fashion, and poked the ground idly with a short stick. "It's still following, Barney," he said. "He must have known that at least one of our boys would have heard of this place and remember it. He purposely picked a place we'd be sure to come to, and on top of that he made it double easy to find."

"Well, you got to admit he'll be fair hard to root out, sittin' on top of that hill. Maybe he just wanted a good advantage."

"He had advantages all along the way. Here's the key, Barney. Did he ever once try to get away?" Travisin sat back and watched the outline of the mountain in the fading light. "Now why the devil did he want to bring us here?" He spoke to himself more than to anyone else.

Fry bit off a chew, packing it into his cheek with his tongue. He mumbled, "You've had more luck figurin' the 'Paches than anyone else. You tell me."

"I can't tell you anything, Barney, but I guess one thing's sure. We're going to play Pillo's game just a little longer." He looked up over Fry's shoulder toward the group of scouts. They sat in a semicircle. All wore breechcloths, long moccasins rolled just below the knees, and red calico bands around jet-black hair. Only their different-colored shirts distinguished them. Ningun wore a blue, cast-off army shirt. A leather belt studded with cartridges crossed it over one shoulder. Travisin beckoned to him. "Hey, Ningun. *Aquí!*"

The Apache squatted next to them silently as Travisin began to draw a map in a bare portion of ground with his stick. "Here's where we are and here's that mountain yonder," he indicated, drawing a circle in the earth. "Now you two get together and tell me what's up there and what's in between." He handed the stick to Fry. "And talk fast; it's getting dark."

Not more than an hour later the sun was well behind the western rim of the Basin. The plan had been laid. Travisin and Ningun gave their revolving pistols a last inspection and strode off casually into the darkness of the valley. It struck de Both that they might have been going for an after-dinner stroll.

They kept to the shadows of the trees and rocks as much as possible, Travisin a few steps behind the Apache, who would never walk more than twenty paces without stopping for what seemed like minutes. And then they would go on after the silence settled and began to sing in their ears. Travisin muttered under his breath at the full moon that splashed its soft light on open areas they had to cross. Ningun would walk slowly to the thinnest reaches of the shadows and then dart across the strips of moonlight. For a few seconds he would be only a dark blur in the moonlight and then would disappear into the next shadow. Travisin was never more than ten paces behind him. Soon they were out of the valley ascending the pine-dotted hill. The sand was soft and loose underfoot, muffling their footsteps, but they went on slowly, making sure of each step. In the silence, a dislodged stone would be like a trumpet blast.

On the crest of the hill, Travisin looked back across the valley. The shadowy bulk of the ridge they had left earlier showed in the moonlight, but there was no sign of life on the shoulder. He had not expected to see any, but there was always the young officer. It took more than one patrol to learn about survival in Apache country.

★ ★ ★

THEY MADE THEIR way down the side of the slope into a rugged country of twisting rock formations and wild clumps of desert growth. The mountain loomed much closer now, a gigantic patch of soft gray streaking down from its peak where the moonlight pressed against it. At first, they progressed much slower than before, for the irregular ground rose and fell away without warning; grotesque desert trees and scattered boulders limited their vision to never more than fifty feet ahead. Though at a slower pace, Ningun went ahead with an assurance that he knew where he was going.

Soon they reached a level, bare stretch that seemed to extend into the darkness without end. Ningun changed his direction to the right for a good five hundred yards, and then turned back toward the mountain and the bare expanse of desert leading toward it. He beckoned to Travisin and slid down the crumbly bank of an arroyo that led out into the desert. In five months it would be a rushing stream, carrying the rain that washed down from the mountain. Now it was a dark path offering a stingy protection up to the door of Pillo's stronghold.

They followed the erratic, weaving course of the arroyo until it turned sharply, as the ground began to rise, and passed out of sight around the southern base of the mountain. The top of the mountain still lay almost a mile above them—up a gradual slope at first, dotted with small trees, then to rougher ground. The last few hundred yards climbed tortuously over steep jagged rock to the mesa above.

Ningun scurried out of the arroyo and disappeared into a small clump of brush a dozen yards away. In a moment his head appeared, and Travisin followed. They crept more cautiously now from cover to cover. A low, mournful sound cut the stillness. Both stopped dead. Travisin waited for Ningun to move, but he remained stone-still for almost five minutes. No sound followed. Ningun shook his head and whispered, "Night bird."

★ ★ ★

He led on, not straight up, but almost parallel with the base of the mountain, climbing gradually all the time. They had almost reached the steeper grade when the Apache pointed ahead to a black slash that cut into the mountain. Going closer, Travisin made out a narrow canyon that reached into the mountain on an upgrade. It was gouged sharply into the side of the mountain and extended crookedly down the slight grade to the desert below. Ahead, it made a bend in the darkness and was lost to sight. They climbed along the rim of the canyon for a few minutes while Travisin studied its course and depth, then they doubled back, climbing steadily up the mountain. A hundred yards further on, the Apache gave Travisin a sign and disappeared into the darkness. He waited for almost twenty minutes, toward the end beginning to wonder about the Indian, and then he looked to the side and saw Ningun approaching only a few feet away.

The Apache pressed one finger to his lips, then whispered to the captain. Travisin nodded and followed him, creeping slowly up the rocky incline above. They reached a wide ledge, Ningun leading along it to the left before climbing again over a shoulder-high hump that stretched into a long, flat piece of ground. Two hundred yards to the right, the mountain rose higher to a craggy peak, sharp and jagged. Nothing would be up there. Travisin and Ningun were on the mesa. Not far away they heard a pony sneeze.

On this part of the mesa the grass was tall. They crawled along, a foot at a time, toward the sound of the pony. The grass made a slight, stirring noise as they crawled through it, but at that height it could easily be the wind. Every few feet they would sink to their stomachs and lie flat in the grass for a matter of minutes, and then go on, extending a hand slowly to a firm portion of ground before dragging up the legs just as slowly. In this way they covered a portion of the mesa that extended to a scattered line of small boulders. The occasional snort of a pony seemed to come from less than a stone's throw away.

Travisin raised his head gradually an inch at a time until he could look between two of the rocks. From there the ground dipped slightly into a shallow pocket, descending from four sides to form a natural barricade. As he peered over the rocks, the moon passed behind a cloud and he could make out only the dying embers of a cook fire in the middle of the area. As the cloud moved on, the moon began to reappear gradually, the soft light crawling over slowly from the right, first illuminating the pony herd and then extending toward the center of the pocket. In a few seconds the entire camp area was bathed in the light. Travisin felt a weight drop through his breast as he counted sixty-three Chiricahuas.

The amazement of it held his gaze between the two rocks for a longer time than he realized. He jerked his head back quickly and looked at Ningun who had been spying the camp from a similar concealment. As he looked at Ningun he realized that the Apache understood now, just as he did, why

Pillo had left such an obvious trail. But this was not the place to discuss it.

Making their way back to the outer edge of the mesa seemed to take even longer, though actually they snaked through the tall grass at a faster pace than before. They were seasoned enough to retain their calm caution, but now time was even more important, if they were to cope with Pillo. In less than two hours the sun would be present to create new problems. At the edge of the mesa Travisin, still crouched, peered cautiously to the ledge below, and then past it, determining the quickest route that would lead them to their planned rendezvous with Fry and the others.

Without speaking, he nudged Ningun and pointed a direction diagonally down the mountainside. The scout rose to his feet silently and placed himself in position to jump to the ledge below. Travisin turned his head for a last look in the direction of the hostile camp. As he did so, he heard a dull thud and an agonizing grunt escape from the scout. He wheeled, instinctively drawing his pistol, and saw Ningun go backward over the edge, an arrow shaft protruding from his chest.

★ ★ ★

TRAVISIN WAS UP and hurling himself at the ledge in one motion. It happened so fast that the Apache aiming his bow on the ledge below was just a blur, but he heard the arrow whine overhead as he landed on the sprawled form of Ningun and was projected off balance toward the Apache a few feet away. The Apache hurled his bow aside with a piercing shriek and went for a knife at his waist just as Travisin brought his pistol up. In the closeness, the front sight caught in the Apache's waistband on the upward swing, and the barrel was pressing into his stomach when he pulled the trigger. The Indian screamed again and staggered back off the ledge. Travisin hesitated a second, searching the mountainside for the best escape, but it was too late. He heard the yelp at the same time he felt the heavy blow at the back of his skull. He heard the wind rush through his ears and saw the orange flash sear across his eyes, and then nothing.

Chapter Six

Pillo waited until the officer opened his eyes and started to prop himself up on his elbows. Then he kicked Travisin in the temple with the side of his moccasined foot. The Indians howled with laughter as Travisin sprawled on his back, shook his head and attempted to rise again. Pillo caught him on the shoulder this time, but still with enough force to slam the officer back against the ground. The other

Apaches closed in, a few of them catching Travisin about the head and shoulders with vicious kicks, before Pillo stepped close to Travisin and held his hands in the air. He chattered for some time in Apache, raising and lowering his voice, and at the end they all stepped back; Pillo was still chief, though wizened and scarred with age. Travisin knew enough of the tongue to know that he was being saved for something else. He thought of old Solomon.

Two of the warriors pulled him to his feet and half-dragged him to the center of the rancheria. Most of the Apaches were stripped to breechcloths, streaks of paint on their chests contrasting with the dinginess of their dirt-smudged bodies. They stood about him, silent now, their dark eyes burning with anticipation of what was to come. Asesino, Pillo's son-in-law, walked up to within a foot of the captain, stared at him momentarily and then spat full in his face. Asesino's lips were curling into laughter when Travisin punched him in the mouth and sent him sprawling at the feet of the warriors.

★ ★ ★

HE ROSE SLOWLY, reaching for his knife, but Pillo again intervened, speaking harshly to his son-in-law. Pillo was the statesman, the general, not a rowdy guerrilla leader. There would be time for blood, but now he must tell this upstart white soldier what the situation was. That it was the Apache's turn.

He began with the usual formality of explaining the Apache position, but went back farther than Cochise and Mangas Coloradas, both in his own lifetime, to list his complaints against the white man. The Apache has no traditional history to fall back on, but Pillo spoke long enough about the last ten years to compare with any plains Indian's war chant covering generations. As he spoke, the other Apaches would grumble or howl, but did not take their eyes from Travisin. The captain stared back at them insolently, his gaze going from one to the next, never dropping his eyes. But he noted more than scowling faces. He saw that though lookouts were posted on the eastern edge of the mesa, the direction from which he and Ningun had come hours before, the western side, was empty of any Apaches.

Pillo was finishing with background now, and becoming more personal. He spoke in a mixture of Spanish and English, relying on Apache when an emphatic point had to be made. He spoke of promises made and broken by the white man. He spoke of Crook, whom the Apache trusted, but who was gone now.

"Look around, white soldier, you see many *Tinneh* here, but you will not live to see the many more that will come. Soon will come Jicarillas, Tontos and many Mescaleros, and the white men will be driven to the north." As he spoke he pushed his open shirt aside and scratched his stomach.

Travisin saw the two animal teeth hanging from his neck by a leather string. It was then that the idea started to form in his mind. It was rash, something he would have laughed at in a cooler moment; but he glanced at the fire that meant torture. He looked across it and saw Gatito. There was the answer! The animal teeth and Gatito.

"Pillo speaks with large mouth, but only wind comes out," Travisin said suddenly, feeling confidence rise at the boldness of his words. "You speak of many things that will happen, but they are all lies, for before any *Tinneh* come I shall drag you and your people back to the reservation, where you will all be punished."

* * *

PILLO STARTED to howl with laughter, but was cut short by Travisin. "Hold your tongue, old man! I do not speak with the wind. U-sen Himself sent me. He knows what your medicine is." Travisin paused for emphasis. "And I am that medicine!"

Pillo's lips formed laughter, but the sound was not there. The white soldier spoke of his medicine.

"All your people know that your medicine is the gray wolf who protects you, because U-sen has always made Himself known through the gray wolf to guard you from evil. I tell you, old man, if you or any warrior lays a hand on me as I leave here, you will be struck dead by U-sen's arrow, the lightning stroke. If you do not believe me, touch me!"

Pillo was unnerved. An Apache's medicine is the most important part of his existence. Not something to be tampered with. Travisin addressed Pillo again, turning toward Gatito.

"If Pillo does not believe, let him ask Gatito if I do not have power from U-sen. Ask Gatito, who was the best stalker in the Army, if he was ever able to even touch me, though he tried many times. Ask him if I am not the wolf."

The renegade scout looked at Travisin wide-eyed. He had never thought of this before, but it must be true! He remembered the dozens of times he had tried to win his bet with the captain. Each time he had been but a few feet away, when the captain had laughed and turned on him. The thought swept through his mind and was given support by his primitive superstitions and instincts. Pillo and the others watched him and they saw that he believed. Travisin saw, and exhaled slowly through clenched teeth.

He turned from Pillo and walked toward the western rim of the mesa without another word. It had to be bold or not at all. Apaches in his way fell back quickly as he walked through the circle and out of the rancheria. His strides were long but unhurried as he made his way through the tall grass, looking straight ahead of him and never once behind.

The flesh on the back of his neck tingled and he hunched his shoulders slightly as if expecting at any moment to feel the smash of a bullet or an arrow. For the hundred yards he walked with this uncertainty, the spring in him winding, tightening to catapult him forward into a driving sprint. But he paced off the yards calmly, fighting back the urge to bolt. Nearing the mesa rim his neck muscles uncoiled, and he took a deep breath of the thin air.

There on the western side, the mesa edge slanted, without an abrupt drop, into the irregular fall of the mountainside. A path stretched from the mesa diagonally down the side to be lost among rocks and small rises that twisted the path right and left down the long slope.

Travisin was only a few feet from the path when the Apache loomed in front of him coming up the trail. Though many things raced through his mind, he stopped dead only a split second before throwing himself at the Apache. They closed, chest to chest, and Travisin could smell the rankness of his body as they went over the rim and rolled down the path to land heavily against a tree stump. Travisin lost his hold on the Indian but landed on top clawing for his throat. A saber-sharp pain cut through his back and his nostrils filled with dust and sweat-smell. The Apache's face was a straining blur below him, the neck muscles stretching like steel cords. He pulled one hand from the Apache's throat, clawed up a rock the size of his fist and brought it down in the Indian's face in one sweeping motion, grinding through bone and flesh to drive the Indian's scream back down his throat.

As he rose to run down the path, the carbine shot ricocheted off the mesa rim above him. His medicine was broken.

☆

Chapter Seven

An hour before dawn Fry had finished spotting his scouts along one side of the narrow canyon that gouged into the shoulder of Pillo's mountain stronghold. One scout was a mile behind with the mounts; the others, concealed among the rocks and brush that climbed the canyon wall, were playing their favorite game. An Apache will squat behind a bush motionless all day to take just one shot at an enemy. Here was the promise of a bountiful harvest. Each man was his own troop, his own company, each knowing how to fight the Apache best, for he is an Apache.

They were to meet Travisin and Ningun there at

dawn and wait. Wait and watch, under the assumption that sooner or later Pillo would lead his band down from the mountain. The logical trail was through the canyon. And the logical place for a jackpot was here where the canyon narrowed to a defile before erupting out to the base of the mountain.

De Both crouched near Fry, watching him closely, studying his easy calm, hoping that the contagion of his indifference would sweep over him and throttle the gnawing fear in his belly. But de Both was an honest man, and his fear was an honest fear. He was just young. His knees trembled not so much at the thought of the coming engagement, his first, but at the question: Would he do the right thing? What would his reaction be? He knew it would make or break him.

And then, before he could prepare himself, it had begun. Two, three, four carbine shots screamed through the canyon, up beyond their sight. At the same time, there was a blur of motion on the opposite canyon wall not a hundred yards away and the Apache came into sight. He leaped from boulder to rock down the steep wall of the canyon until he was on level ground. He gazed for a few seconds in the direction from which the shots had come, then crossed the canyon floor at a trot and started to scale the other wall from which he would have a better command of the extending defile. He stopped and crouched behind a rock not twenty feet below de Both's position. Then he turned and began to climb again.

★ ★ ★

OFTEN WHEN YOU haven't time to think, you're better off, your instinct takes over and your body follows through. De Both pressed against the boulder in front of him feeling the coolness of it on his cheek, pushing his knees tight against the ground. He heard the loose earth crumble under the Apache's moccasins as he neared the rock. He heard the Indian's hand pat against the smooth surface of it as he reached for support. And as his heart hammered in his chest the urge to run made his knees quiver and his boot moved with a spasmodic scrape. It cut the stillness like a knife dragged across an emery stone, and it shot de Both to his feet to look full into the face of the Apache.

Asesino tried to bring his carbine up, but he was too late. De Both's arms shot across the narrow rock between them and his fingers dug into the Apache's neck. Asesino fell back, pushing his carbine lengthwise against the blue jacket with a force that dragged the officer over the rock on top of him, and they writhed on the slope, their heads pointing to the canyon floor. The Indian tried to yell, but fingers, bone-white with pressure, gouged vocal cords and only a gurgling squeak passed agonized lips. His arms thrashed wildly, tore at the back of the blue jacket and a hand crawled downward to unexpectedly clutch the bone handle of the knife. Light flashed on the blade as it rose in the air and plunged into the straining blue cloth.

★ ★ ★

THERE WAS A GASP, an air-sucking moan. De Both rolled from the Apache with his eyes stretched open to see Fry's boot crush against the Indian's cheekbone. His eyes closed then and he felt the burning between his shoulder blades. He felt Fry's hands tighten at his armpits to pull him back up the slope behind the rock. The same hands tore shirt and tunic to the collar and then gently untied the grimy neckerchief to pad it against the wound.

"You ain't bad hurt, mister. You didn't leave enough strength in him to do a good job." And his heavy tobacco breath brushed against the officer's cheek and made him turn his head.

"I feel all right. But . . . what about the blood?"

"I'll fix you up later, mister. No time now. The captain's put in an appearance." He jerked a thumb over his shoulder.

Far down the canyon a lone figure ran, his arms pumping, his head thrown back, mouth sucking in air. It was a long, easy lope paced to last miles without let-up. It was the pace of a man who ran, but knew what he was doing. Death was behind, but the trail was long. As he came nearer to the scouts' positions, Fry raised slightly and gave a low, shrill whistle, then cut it off abruptly. Travisin glanced up the canyon slope without slacking his pace and passed into the shadows of the defile just as the Apaches trickled from the rocks three hundred yards up the canyon. They saw him pass into the narrowness as they swept onto the canyon floor, over fifty strong, screaming down the passage like a cloud of vampires beating from a cavern. Their yells screeched against the canyon walls and whiplashed back and forth in the narrowness.

Fry sighted down his Remington-Hepburn waiting for the hostiles to come abreast. He turned his head slightly and cut a stream of tobacco into the sand. "Captain was sure right about their sign. They was pavin' us a road clean to hell. Have to find out sometime where they all come from." He squinted down the short barrel, his finger taking in the slack on the trigger. "In about one second you can make all the noise you want." The barrel lifted slightly with the explosion and a racing Apache was knocked from his feet. A split second later, nine more carbines blasted into the canyon bottom.

Fry was on his feet after the first shot, pumping bullets into the milling mass of brown bodies as fast as he could squeeze the trigger. The hostiles had floundered at the first shot, tripping, knocking each other down in an effort to reach safety, but they didn't know where to turn. They were caught in their own kind of trap. They screamed, and danced about frantically. A few tried to rush up the slope into the mouth of the murderous fire from the scouts, but they were cut down at once. Others tried to scale the opposite wall, but the steep slope was slow going and they were picked off easily. They dashed about in a circle firing wildly at the canyon wall, wasting their ammunition on small puffs of smoke that rose above the rocks and brush clumps. And they kept dropping, one at a time. Five shots in succession, two, then one. The last bullet scream died away up-canyon. There was the beginning of silence, but almost immediately the air was pierced with a new sound. Throats shrieked again, but with a vigor, with a lust. It was not the agonized scream of the terrified Chiricahua, but the battle yell of the Coyotero scout as he hurled himself down the slope into the enemy. They had earned their army pay; now it was time for personal vengeance.

Half of the hostiles threw their arms into the air as the scouts swarmed into the open, but they came on with knives and gun stocks raised. Savage closed with savage in a grinding melee of thrashing arms and legs in thick dust, the cornered animal, made more ferocious by his fear, battling the hunter who had tasted blood. They came back with their knives dripping, their carbine stocks shattered.

★ ★ ★

IT TOOK TWO DAYS longer to return to the little subagency on the banks of the Gila, because it is slower travel with wounded men and sixteen Chiricahua hostiles whose legs are roped under the horses' bellies by day and whose hands are lashed to trees by night. Travisin led and was silent.

De Both held himself tense against the searing pain that shot up between his shoulder blades. But oddly enough, he did not really mind the ride home. He looked at the line of sixteen hostiles and felt nothing. No hate. No pity. Slowly it came upon him that it was indifference, and he moved his stained hat to a cockier angle. Boston could be a million miles away and he could be at the end of the earth, but de Both didn't particularly give a damn. He knew he was a man.

Fry chewed tobacco while his listless eyes swept the ground for a sign. That's what he was paid for. It kept running through his mind that it was an awful funny thing to go out after sixteen hostiles, meet sixty and still come back with sixteen. Have to tell that one at Lon Scorey's in Globe.

Pillo rode with his chin on his bony chest. He was much older, and the throbbing hole in his thigh didn't help him, either. He was beginning to smell the greenness of decay.

On the afternoon of the fourth day they rode slowly into the quadrangle at Gila. Travisin looked about. Nothing had changed. For a moment he had expected to find something different, and he yearned for something that wasn't there. But he threw aside his longing and slumped back into his role—the role that forced him to be the best Apache campaigner in the Territory.

A cavalry mount stood in front of the agency office and a trooper appeared on the porch as Travisin, Fry and de Both dismounted and walked to the welcome shade of the ramada.

"Compliments of the commanding officer, sir. I've rode from Fort Thomas with this message."

Travisin read the note and turned with a smile to the other two. "Bill, let me tell you one thing if you don't already know it. Never try to figure out the ways of a woman—or the army. This is from Collier. He says the Bureau has decided to return Pillo and his band to his people at Fort Apache. All sixteen of 'em. Certainly is a good thing we've got sixteen to send back."

Fry said, "Yep, you might have got yourself court-martialed. Way it is, if Pillo loses that leg, you'll probably end up back as a looie."

De Both listened and the quizzical look turned to anger. He opened his mouth to speak, but thought better of it and waited until he had cooled off before muttering simply, "Idiots!"

If Travisin was the winking type, he would have looked at Fry and done so. He glanced at Fry with the hint of a smile, but with eyes that said, "Barney, I think we've got ourselves a lieutenant." Then he walked into the office. There are idiotic Bureau decisions, and there are boots that have been on too long.

And along the Gila, the war drums are silent again. But on frontier station, you don't relax. For though they are less in number, they are still Apaches.

2

You Never See Apaches . . .

By nature, Angsman was a cautious man. From the shapeless specks that floated in the sky miles out over the plain, his gaze dropped slowly to the sand a few feet from his chin, then rose again more slowly, to follow the gradual slope that fell away before him. He rolled his body slightly from its prone position to reach the field glasses at his side, while his eyes continued to crawl out into the white-hot nothingness of the flats. Sun glare met alkali dust and danced before the slits of his eyes. And, far out, something moved. Something darker than the monotonous tone of the flats. A pinpoint of motion.

He put the glasses to his eyes and the glare stopped dancing and the small blur of motion cleared and enlarged as he corrected the focus. Two ponies and two pack animals. The mules were loaded high. He made that out right away, but it was minutes before he realized the riders were women. Two Indian women. Behind them the scavenger birds floated above the scattered animal carcasses, circling lower as the human figures moved away.

Angsman pushed himself up from the sand and made his way back through the pines that closed in on the promontory. A few dozen yards of the darkness of the pines and then abruptly the glare was forcing against sand again where the openness of the trail followed the shoulder of the hill. He stopped at the edge of the trees, took his hat off, and rubbed the red line where the sweatband had stuck. His mustache drooped untrimmed toward dark, tight cheeks, giving his face a look of sadness. A stern, sun-scarred sadness. It was the type of face that needed the soft shadow of a hat brim to make it look complete. Shadows to soften the gaunt angles. It was an intelligent, impassive face, in its late thirties. He looked at the three men by the horses and then moved toward them.

Ygenio Baca sat cross-legged in the dust smoking a cigarette, drawing deep, and he only glanced at Angsman as he approached. He drew long on his cigarette, then held it close to his eyes and examined it as some rare object as the smoke curled from his mouth. Ygenio Baca, the mozo, had few concerns.

Ed Hyde's stocky frame was almost beneath his horse's head, with a hand lifted to the horse's muzzle. The horse's nose moved gently against the big palm, licking the salty perspiration from hand and wrist. In the other arm Hyde cradled a Sharps rifle. His squinting features were obscure beneath the hat tilted close to his eyes. Sun, wind, and a week's beard gave his face a puffy, raw appearance that was wild, but at the same time soft and hazy. There was about him a look of sluggishness that contrasted with the leanness of Angsman.

Billy Guay stood indolently with his thumbs hooked in his gun belts. He took a few steps in Angsman's direction and pushed his hat to the back of his head, though the sun was beating full in his face. He was half Ed Hyde's age, a few years or so out of his teens, but there was a hardness about the eyes that contrasted with his soft features. Features that were all the more youthful, and even feminine, because of the long blond hair that covered the tops of his ears and hung unkempt over his shirt collar. Watching Angsman, his mouth was tight as if daring him to say something that he would not agree with.

Angsman walked past him to Ed Hyde. He was about to say something, but stopped when Billy Guay turned and grabbed his arm.

"The dust cloud was buffalo like I said, wasn't it?" Billy Guay asked, but there was more statement of fact than question in his loud voice.

Angsman's serious face turned to the boy, but looked back to Ed Hyde when he said, "There're two Indian women out there cleaning up after a hunting party. The dust cloud was the warriors going home. I suspect they're the last ones. Stragglers. Everyone else out of sight already."

Billy Guay pushed in close to the two men. "Dammit, the cloud could have still been buffalo," he said. "Who says you know so damn much!"

Ed Hyde looked from one to the other like an unbiased spectator. He dropped the long buffalo rifle stock down in front of him. His worn black serge coat strained tight at the armpits as he lifted his hands to pat his coat pockets. From the right one he drew a half-chewed tobacco plug.

For a moment Angsman just stared at Billy Guay. Finally he said, "Look, boy, for a good many years it's been my business to know so damn much. Now, you'll take my word that the dust cloud was an Indian hunting party and act on it like I see fit, or else we turn around and go back."

Ed Hyde's grizzled head jerked up suddenly. He said, "You're dead right, Angsman. There ain't been buffalo this far south for ten years." He looked at the boy and spoke easier. "Take my word for it, Billy." He smiled. "If anybody knows it, I do. Those Indians most likely ran down a deer herd. But hell, deer, buffalo, what's the difference? We're not out here for game. You just follow along with what Angsman here says and we all go home rich men. Take things slow, Billy, and you breathe easier."

"I just want to know why's he got to give all the orders," Billy Guay said, and his voice was rising. "It's us that own the map, not him. Where'd he be without us!"

Angsman's voice was the same, unhurried, unexcited, when he said, "I'll tell you. I'd still be back at Bowie guiding for cavalry who ride with their eyes open and know how to keep their mouths shut in Apache country." He didn't wait for a reply, but turned and walked toward the dun-colored mare. "Ygenio," he called to the Mexican still sitting cross-legged on the ground, "hold the mules a good fifty yards behind us and keep your eyes on me."

* * *

EIGHT DAYS OUT of Willcox and the strain was beginning to tell. It had been bad from the first day. Now they were in the foothills of the Mogollons and it was no better. Angsman had thought that as soon as they climbed from the dust of the plains the tension would ease and the boy would be easier to handle, but Billy Guay continued to grumble with his thumbs in his gun belts and disagree with everything that was said. And Ed Hyde continued to say nothing unless turning back was mentioned.

Since early morning their trail had followed this pine-covered crest that angled irregularly between the massive rock peaks to the south and east and the white-gold plain to the west. Most of the ways the trail had held to the shoulder, turning, twisting, and falling with the contour of the hillcrest. And from the west the openness of the plains continued to cling in glaring monotony. Most of the time Angsman's eyes scanned the openness, and the small black specks continued to crawl along in his vision.

The trail dipped abruptly into a dry creek basin that slanted down from between rocky humps looming close to the right. Angsman reined his mount diagonally down the bank, then at the bottom kicked hard to send the mare into a fast start up the opposite bank. The gravel loosened and fell away as hooves dug through the dry crust to clink against the sandy rock. Momentarily the horse began to fall back, but Angsman spurred again and grunted something close to her ear to make the mare heave and kick up over the bank.

He rode on a few yards before turning to wait for the others.

Billy Guay reached the creek bank and yelled across, without hesitating, "Hey, Angsman, you tryin' to pick the roughest damn trail you can find?"

The scout winced as the voice slammed against the towering rock walls and drifted over the flats, vibrating and repeating far off in the distance. He threw off and ran to the creek bank. Billy Guay began to laugh as the echo came back to him. "Damn, Ed. You hear that!" His voice carried clear and loud across the arroyo. Angsman put a finger to his mouth and shook his head repeatedly when he saw Ed Hyde looking his way. Then Hyde leaned close and said something to the boy. He heard Billy Guay swear, but not so loud, and then there was silence.

Now, ten days from the time the message had brought him to the hotel in Willcox, he wasn't so sure it was worth it.

In the hotel room Hyde had come to the point immediately. Anxiety showed on his face, but he smiled when he asked the point-blank question "How'd you like to be worth half a hundred thousand dollars?" With that he waved the piece of dirty paper in front of Angsman's face. "It's right here. Find us the picture of a Spanish sombrero and we're rich." That simply.

Angsman had all the time in the world. He

smoked a cigarette and thought. Then he asked, "Why me? There're a lot of prospectors around here."

Hyde did something with his eye that resembled a wink. "You're well recommended here in Willcox. They say you know the country better than most. And the Apaches better than anybody," Hyde said with a hint of self-pride for knowing so much about the scout. "Billy here and I'll give you an equal share of everything we find if you can guide us to one little X on a piece of paper."

Billy Guay had said little that first meeting. He half-sat on the small window ledge trying to stare Angsman down when the scout looked at him. And Angsman smiled when he noticed the boy's two low-slung pistols, thinking a man must be a pretty poor shot with one pistol that he'd have to carry another. And when Billy Guay tried to stare him down, he stared back with the half smile and it made the boy all the madder; so mad that often, then, he interrupted Hyde to let somebody know that he had something to say about the business at hand.

Ed Hyde told a story of a lost mine and a prospector who had found the mine, but was unable to take any gold out because of Indians, and who was lucky to get out with just his skin. He referred to the prospector always as "my friend," and finally it turned out that "my friend" was buffalo hunting out of Tascosa in the Panhandle, along with Ed Hyde, raising a stake to try the mine again, when he "took sick and died." The two of them were out on a hunt when it happened and he left the map to Hyde, "since I saw him through his sickness." Ed Hyde remained silent for a considerable length of time after telling of the death of his friend.

Then he added, "I met Billy here later on and took to him 'cause he's got the nerve for this kind of business." He looked at Billy Guay as a man looks at a younger man and sees his own youth. "Just one thing more, mister," he added. "If you say yes and look at the map, you don't leave our sight."

In the Southwest, lost-mine stories are common. Angsman had heard many, and knew even more prospectors who chased the legends. He had seen a few become rich. But it wasn't so much the desire for gold that finally prompted him to go along. Cochise had promised peace and Geronimo had scurried south to the Sierra Madres. All was quiet in his territory. Too quiet. He had told himself he would go merely as an escape from boredom. Still, it was hard to keep the wealth aspect from cropping into the thought. Angsman saw the years slipping by with nothing to show for them but a scarred Spanish saddle and an old-model Winchester. All he had to do was lead them to a canyon and a rock formation that looked like a Spanish hat.

Two days to collect the equipment and round up a mozo who wasn't afraid to drive mules into that part of Apacheria where there was no peace. For cigarettes and a full belly Ygenio Baca would drive his mules to the gates of hell.

★ ★ ★

IT WAS ALMOST a mile past the arroyo crossing that Angsman noticed his black specks had disappeared from the open flats. For the past few hundred yards his vision to the left had been blocked by dense pines. Now the plains yawned wide again, and his glasses inched over the vastness in all directions, then stopped where a spur jutted out from the hillside ahead to cut his vision. The Indian women had vanished.

Hyde and Billy Guay sat their mounts next to Angsman, who, afoot, swept his glasses once more over the flat. Finally he lowered them and said, more to himself than to the others, "Those Indian women aren't nowhere in sight. They could have moved out in the other direction, or they might be so close we can't see them."

He nodded ahead to where the trail stopped at thick scrub brush and pine and then dipped abruptly to the right to drop to a bench that slanted toward the deepness of the valley. From where they stood, the men saw the trail disappear far below into a denseness of trees and rock.

"Pretty soon the country'll be hugging us tight; and we won't see anything," Angsman said. "I don't like it. Not with a hunting party in the neighborhood."

Billy Guay laughed out. "I'll be go to hell! Ed, this old woman's afraid of two squaws! Ed, you hear—"

Ed Hyde wasn't listening. He was staring off in the distance, past the treetops in the valley to a towering, sand-colored cliff with flying rock buttresses that walled the valley on the other side. He slid from his mount hurriedly, catching his coat on the saddle horn and ripping it where a button held fast. But now he was too excited to heed the ripped coat.

"Look! Yonder to that cliff." His voice broke with excitement. "See that gash near the top, like where there was a rock slide? And look past to the mountains behind!" Angsman and Billy Guay squinted at the distance, but remained silent.

"Dammit!" Hyde screamed. "Don't you see it!" He grabbed his horse's reins and ran, stumbling, down the trail to where it leveled again at the bench. When the others reached him, the map was in his hand and he was laughing a high laugh that didn't seem to belong to the grizzled face. His extended hand held the dirty piece of paper . . . and he kept jabbing at it with a finger of the other hand. "Right there, dammit! Right there!" His pointing finger swept from the map. "Now look at that gold-lovin' rock slide!" His laughter subsided to a self-confident chuckle.

From where they stood on the bench, the towering cliff was now above them and perhaps a mile away over the tops of the trees. A chunk of sandrock as large as a two-story building was gouged from along the smooth surface of the cliff top, with a gravel slide trailing into the valley below; but massive boulders along the cliff top lodged over the depression, forming a four-sided opening. It was a gigantic frame through which they could see sky and the flat surface of a mesa in the distance. On both sides the mesa top fell away to shoulders cutting sharp right angles from the straight vertical lines, then to be cut off there, in their vision, by the rock border of the cliff frame. And before their eyes the mesa turned into a flat-topped Spanish sombrero.

Billy Guay's jaw dropped open. "Damn! It's one of those hats like the Mex dancers wear! Ed, you see it?"

Ed Hyde was busy studying the map. He pointed to it again. "Right on course, Angsman. The flats, the ridge, the valley, the hat." His black-crusted fingernail followed wavy lines and circles over the stained paper. "Now we just drop to the valley and follow her up to the end." He shoved the map into his coat pocket and reached up to the saddle horn to mount. "Come on, boys, we're good as rich," he called, and swung up into the saddle.

Angsman looked down the slant to the darkness of the trees. "Ed, we got to go slow down there," he tried to caution, but Hyde was urging his mount down the grade and Billy Guay's paint was kicking the loose rock after him. His face tightened as he turned quickly to his horse, and then he saw Ygenio Baca leaning against his lead mule vacantly smoking his cigarette. Angsman's face relaxed.

"Ygenio," he said. "Tell your mules to be very quiet."

Ygenio Baca nodded and unhurriedly flicked the cigarette stub down the grade.

They caught up with Hyde and Billy Guay a little way into the timber. The trail had disappeared into a hazy gloom of tangled brush and tree trunks with the cliff on one side and the piney hill on the other to keep out the light.

Angsman rode past them and they stopped and turned in the saddle. Hyde looked a little sheepish because he didn't know where the trail was, but Billy Guay stared back defiantly and tried to look hard.

"Ed, you saw some bones out there on the flats a while back," Angsman said. "Likely they were men who had gold fever." That was all he said. He turned the head of the mare and continued on.

Angsman moved slowly, more cautiously now than before, and every so often he would rein in gently and sit in the saddle without moving, and listen. And there was something about the deep silence that made even Billy Guay strain his eyes into the dimness and not say anything. It was a loud quietness that rang in their ears and seemed unnatural. Moving at this pace, it was almost dusk when they reached the edge of the timber.

The pine hill was still on their left, but higher and steeper. To the right, two spurs reached out from the cliff wall that had gradually dropped until now it was just a hump, but with a confusion of rocky angles in the near distance beyond. And ahead was a canyon mouth, narrow at first, but then appearing to open into a wider area.

As they rode on, Angsman could see it in Ed Hyde's eyes. The map was in his hand and he kept glancing at it and then looking around. When they passed through the canyon mouth into the open, Hyde called, "Angsman, look! Just like it says!"

But Angsman wasn't looking at Ed Hyde. A hundred feet ahead, where a narrow side canyon cut into the arena, the two Indian women sat their ponies and watched the white men approach.

★ ★ ★

ANGSMAN REINED in and waited, looking at them the way you look at deer that you have come across unexpectedly in a forest, waiting for them to bolt. But the women made no move to run. Hyde and Billy Guay drew up next to Angsman, then continued on as Angsman nudged the mare into a walk.

They stopped within a few feet of the women, who had still neither moved nor uttered a sound.

Angsman dismounted. Hyde stirred restlessly in his saddle before putting his hands on the horn to swing down, but stopped when Billy Guay's hand tightened on his arm.

"Damn, Ed, look at that young one!" His voice was loud and excited, but as impersonal as if he were making a comment at a girlie show. "She'd even look good in town," he added, and threw off to stand in front of her pony.

Angsman looked at Billy Guay and back to the girl, who was sliding easily from the bare back of her pony. He greeted her in English, pleasantly, and tipped his hat to the older woman, still mounted, who giggled in a high, thin voice. The girl said nothing, but looked at Angsman.

He said, *¿Cómo se llama?* and spoke a few more words in Spanish.

The girl's face relaxed slightly and she said, "Sonkadeya," pronouncing each syllable distinctly.

"What the hell's that mean?" Billy Guay said, walking up to her.

"That's her name," Angsman told him, then spoke to the girl again in Spanish.

She replied with a few Spanish phrases, but most of her words were in a dialect of the Apache tongue. She was having trouble combining the two languages so that the white men could understand her. Her face would frown and she would wipe her hands nervously over the hips of her greasy deerskin dress as she groped for the right words. She was plump and her hair and dress had long gone unwashed, but her face was softly attractive, contrasting oddly with her primitive dress and speech. Her features might have belonged to a white woman—the coloring, too, for that matter—but the greased hair and smoke smell that clung to her were decidedly Apache.

When she finished speaking, Angsman looked back at Hyde. "She's a Warm Springs Apache. A Mimbreño," he said. "She says they're on their way home."

Hyde said, "Ask her if she knows about any gold hereabouts."

Angsman looked at him and his eyes opened a little wider. "Maybe you didn't hear, Ed. I said she's a Mimbre. She's going home from a hunting trip led by her father. And her father's Delgadito," he added.

"Hell, the 'Paches are at peace, ain't they?" Hyde asked indifferently. "What you worried about?"

"Cochise made peace," Angsman answered. "These are Mimbres, not Chiricahuas, and their chief is Victorio. He's never never made peace. I don't want to scare you, Ed," he said looking back to the girl, "but his war lieutenant's Delgadito."

Billy Guay was standing in front of the girl, his

thumbs in his gun belts, looking at her closely. "I know how to stop a war," he said, smiling.

"Who's talkin' about war?" Hyde asked. "We're not startin' anything."

"You don't have to stop it, Ed," Angsman said. "You think about finishing it. And you think about your life."

"Don't worry about me thinkin' about my life. I think about it bein' almost gone and not worth a Dixie single. Hell, yes, we're takin' a chance!" Hyde argued. "If gold was easy to come by, it wouldn't be worth nothin'."

"I still know how to stop a war," Billy Guay said idly.

Hyde looked at him impatiently. "What's that talk supposed to mean?" Then he saw how Billy Guay was looking at the girl, and the frown eased off the grizzled face as it dawned on him what Billy Guay was thinking about, and he rubbed his beard. "You see what I mean, Ed," Billy Guay said, smiling. "We take Miss Indin along and ain't no Delgadito or even U.S. Grant goin' to stop us." He looked up at the old woman on the pony. "Though I don't see any reason for carryin' excess baggage."

Angsman caught him by both arms and spun him around. "You gun-crazy kid, you out of your mind? You don't wave threats at Apaches!" He pushed the boy away roughly. "Just stop a minute, Ed. You got better sense than what this boy's proposing."

"It's worth a chance, Angsman. Any chance. We're not stoppin' after comin' this far on account of some Indin or his little girl," Hyde said. "I'd say Billy's got the right idea. I told you he had nerve. Let him use a little of it."

Billy Guay looked toward Angsman's mount and saw his handgun in a saddle holster, then both pistols came out and he pointed them at the scout.

"Don't talk again, Angsman, 'cause if I hear any more abuse I'll shoot you as quick as this." He raised a pistol and swung it to the side as if without aiming and pulled the trigger. The old Indian woman dropped from the pony without a cry.

There was silence. Hyde looked at him, stunned. "God, Billy! You didn't have to do that!"

Billy Guay laughed, but the laugh trailed off too quickly, as if he just then realized what he had done. He forced the laugh now, and said, "Hell, Ed. She was only an Indin. What you fussin' about?"

Hyde said, "Well, it's done now and can't be undone." But he looked about nervously as if expecting a simple solution to be standing near at hand. A solution or some kind of justification. He saw the mining equipment packed on one of the mules and the look of distress left his eyes. "Let's quit talkin' about it," he said. "We got things to do."

Billy Guay blew down the barrel of the pistol he had fired and watched Sonkadeya as she bent over the woman momentarily, then rose without the trace of an emotion on her face. It puzzled Billy Guay and made him more nervous. He waved a pistol toward Ygenio Baca. "Hey, Mazo! Get a shovel and turn this old woman under. No sense in havin' the birds tellin' on us."

* * *

THE SCOUT RODE in silence, knowing what would come, but not knowing when. His gaze crawled over the wildness of the slanting canyon walls, brush trees, and scattered boulders, where nothing moved. The left wall was dark, the shadowy rock outlines obscure and blending into each other; the opposite slope was hazy and cold in the dim light of the late sun. He felt the tenseness all over his body. The feeling of knowing that something is close, though you can't see it or hear it. Only the quietness, the metallic clop of hooves, then Billy Guay's loud, forced laughter that would cut the stillness and hang there in the narrowness until it faded out up-canyon. Angsman knew the feeling. It went with campaigning. But this time there was a difference. It was the first time he had ever led into a canyon with such a strong premonition that Apaches were present. Yet, with the feeling, he recognized an eager expectancy. Perhaps fatalism, he thought.

He watched two chicken hawks dodging, gliding in and out, drop toward a brush tree halfway up the slanting right wall, then, just as they were about to land in the bush, they rose quickly and soared out of sight. Now he was more than sure. They were riding into an ambush. And there was so little time to do anything about it.

He glanced at Hyde riding next to him. Hyde couldn't be kept back now. The final circle on his map was just a little figuring from the end of the canyon.

"Slow her down, Ed," Billy Guay yelled. "I can't propose to Miss Indin and canter at the same time." He laughed and reached over to put his hand on Sonkadeya's hip, then let the hand fall to her knee.

He called out, "Yes, sir, Ed, I think we made us a good move."

Sonkadeya did not resist. Her head nodded faintly with the sway of her pony, looking straight ahead. But her eyes moved from one canyon wall to the other and there was the slightest gleam of a smile.

Angsman wondered if he really cared what was going to happen. He didn't care about Hyde or Billy Guay; and he didn't know Ygenio Baca well enough to have a feeling one way or the other. From the beginning Ygenio had been taking a chance like everyone else. He thought of his own life and the odd fact occurred to him that he didn't even particularly care about himself. He tried to picture death in relation to himself, but he would see himself lying on the ground and himself looking at the body and knew that couldn't be so. He thought of how hard it was to take yourself out of the picture to see yourself dead, and ended up with: If you're not going to be there to worry about yourself being dead, why worry at all? But you don't stay alive not caring, and his eyes went back to the canyon sides.

He watched Hyde engrossed in his map and looked back at Billy Guay riding close to Sonkadeya with his hand on her leg. They could be shot from their saddles and not even see where it came from. Or, they could be taken by surprise. His head swung front again and he saw the canyon up ahead narrow to less than fifty feet across. Or they could be taken by surprise!

He flicked the rein against the mare's mane, gently, to ease her toward the right canyon wall. He made the move slowly, leading the others at a very slight angle, so that Hyde and Billy Guay, in their preoccupation, did not even notice the edging. Either to be shot in the head or not at all, Angsman thought.

Now they were riding much closer to the slanting canyon wall. He turned in the saddle to watch Billy Guay, still laughing and moving his hand over Sonkadeya. And when he turned back he saw the half-dozen Apaches standing in the trail not a dozen yards ahead. It was funny, because he was looking at half-naked, armed Apaches and he could still hear Billy Guay's laughter coming from behind.

Then the laughter stopped. Hyde groaned, "Oh, my God!" and in the instant spurred his mount and yanked rein to wheel off to the left. There was the report of a heavy rifle and horse and rider went down.

Angsman's arms were jerked suddenly behind his back and he saw three Apaches race for the fallen Hyde as he felt himself dragged over the rump of the mare. He landed on his feet and staggered and watched one warrior dragging Hyde back toward them by one leg. Hyde was screaming, holding on to the other leg that was bouncing over the rough ground.

Billy Guay had jerked his arms free and stood a little apart from the dozen Apaches aiming bows and carbines at him. His hands were on the pistol butts, with fear and indecision plain on his face.

Angsman twisted his neck toward him, "Don't even think about it, boy. You don't have a chance." It was all over in something like fifteen seconds.

Hyde was writhing on the ground, groaning and holding on to the hole in his thigh, where the heavy slug had gone through to take the horse in the belly. Angsman stooped to look at the wound and saw that Hyde was holding the map, pressed tight to his leg and now smeared with blood. He looked up and Delgadito was standing on the other side of the wounded man. Next to him stood Sonkadeya.

★ ★ ★

DELGADITO WAS NOT dressed for war. He wore a faded red cotton shirt, buttonless and held down by the cartridge belt around his waist; and his thin face looked almost ridiculous under the shabby wide-brimmed hat that sat straight on the top of his head, at least two sizes too small. But Angsman did not laugh. He knew Delgadito, Victorio's war lieutenant, and probably the most capable hit-and-run guerrilla leader in Apacheria. No, Angsman did not laugh.

Delgadito stared at them, taking his time to look around, then said, "Hello. Angs-mon. You have a cigarillo?"

Angsman fished in his shirt pocket and drew out tobacco and paper and handed it to the Indian. Delgadito rolled a cigarette awkwardly and handed the sack to Angsman, who rolled himself one then flicked a match with his thumbnail and lighted the cigarettes. Both men drew deeply and smoked in silence. Finally, Angsman said, "It is good to smoke with you again, Sheekasay."

Delgadito nodded his head and Angsman went on, "It has been five years since we smoked together at San Carlos."

The Apache shook his head slightly. "Together we have smoked other things since then, Angs-mon," and added a few words in the Mimbre dialect.

Angsman looked at him quickly. "You were at Big Dry Wash?"

Delgadito smiled for the first time and nodded his head. "How is your sickness, Angs-mon?" he asked, and the smile broadened.

Angsman's hand came up quickly to his side, where the bullet had torn through that day two years before at Dry Wash, and now he smiled.

Delgadito watched him with the nearest an Apache comes to giving an admiring look. He said, "You are a big man, Angs-mon. I like to fight you. But now you do something very foolish and I must stop you. I mean you no harm, Angs-mon, for I like to fight you, but now you must go home and stop this being foolish and take this old man before the smell enters his leg. And, Angs-mon, tell this old man what befalls him if he returns. Tell him the medicine he carries in his hand is false. Show him how he cannot read the medicine ever again because of his own blood." For a moment his eyes lifted to the heights of the canyon wall. "Maybeso that is the only way, Angs-mon. With blood."

Angsman offered no thanks for their freedom, gratitude was not an Apache custom, but he said, "On the way home I will impress your words on them."

"Tell my words to the old man," Delgadito replied, then his voice became cold. "I will tell the young one." And he looked toward Billy Guay.

Angsman swallowed hard to remain impassive. "There is nothing I can say."

"The mother of Sonkadeya speaks in my ear, Angs-mon. What could you say?" Delgadito turned deliberately and walked away.

Angsman rode without speaking, listening to Hyde's groans as the saddle rubbed the open rawness of his wound. The groans were beginning to erase the scream that hung in his mind and repeated over and over, Billy Guay's scream as they carried him up-canyon.

Angsman knew what he was going to do. He'd still have his worn saddle and old-model carbine, but he knew what he was going to do. Hyde's leg would heal and he'd be back the next year, or the year after; or if not him, someone else. The Southwest was full of Hydes. And as long as there were Hydes, there were Billy Guays. Big talkers with big guns who ended up lying dead, after a while, in a Mimbre rancheria. Angsman would go back to Fort Bowie. Even if it got slow sometimes, there'd always be plenty to do.

3

The Colonel's Lady

Mata Lobo was playing his favorite game. He stretched his legs stiffly behind him until his moccasined feet touched rock, and then he pushed, writhing his body against the soft, sandy ground, enjoying an animal pleasure from the blistering sun on his naked back and the feel of warm, yielding earth beneath him. His extended hand touched the stock of the Sharps rifle a few inches from his chin and sighted down the barrel for the hundredth time. The target area had not changed.

Sixty yards down the slope the military road came into view from between the low hills, cutting a sharp, treacherous arc to follow the bend of Banderas Creek on the near side and then to continue, paralleling the base of the hill, making the slow climb over this section of the Sierra Apaches. Mata Lobo's front sight was dead on the sudden bend in the road.

He flexed his finger on the trigger and sighted again, taking in the slack, then releasing it. Not long now. In a few minutes he should hear the faint, faraway rattle of the stage as it weaved across the plain from Rindo's Station at the Banderas Crossing. Six miles across straight, flat desert. And then louder—with a creaking—a grinding, jingling explosion of leather, wood, and horseflesh as the Hatch & Hodges Overland began the gradual climb over the woody western end of the Sierra Apaches, and then to drop to another white-hot plain that stretched the twelve miles to Inspiration, the end of the line. The vision in the mind of Mata Lobo shortened the route by a dozen miles.

Every foot of the road was known to him. Especially this sudden bend at the beginning of the climb. He had scouted it for weeks, timing the stage runs, watching the drivers from his niche on the hill. And through his Apache patience he learned many things.

At the bend, the driver and the shotgun rider were too busy with the team to be watching the hillside. And the passengers, full and comfortable after a meal at Rindo's, would be suddenly jolted into hanging on with the sway of the bouncing Concord as it swept around the sharp curve, with no thought of looking out the windows.

It was the perfect site for ambush, Apache style. Mata Lobo was sure, for he had done it before.

And then it began. He raised himself on his elbows and cocked his ears to the sound that was still a whisper out on the desert. Two miles away. Then louder, and louder; then the straining pitch to the rattling clamor and the stage was starting up the grade.

The Apache pivoted his rifle on the rocks in front of him, making sure of free motion, and then he lined up again the five brass cartridges arranged on the ground near his right hand.

When he looked back to the road the lead horses were coming into view. He waited until the stage was in full sight, slowed down slightly in the middle of the road, and then he fired, aiming at the closer lead horse.

The horse's momentum carried it along for the space of time it took the Apache to inject another cartridge and squeeze off at the other lead animal. The horses swerved against each other, still going, then four pairs of legs buckled at once, and eight other pairs raced on, trampling the fallen horses, but to be tripped immediately in a wild confusion of thrashing legs and screaming horses and grinding brakes.

Next to the driver the shotgun rider was throwing his boot against the brake lever when the coach jackknifed and twisted over, gouging into the dirt road, sending up a thick cloud of dust to cover the scene.

As the dust began to settle, Mata Lobo saw one figure lying next to the overturned Concord, his face upturned to the two right-side wheels, still turning slowly above him. There was a stir of motion farther ahead as a figure crawled along the ground, got to his feet, stumbled, pulled himself frantically across the road in a wild, reeling motion that finally developed into a crouched run. He was almost to the shelter of the creek bank when the buffalo gun screamed again across the hillsides. The impact threw him over the bank to lie facedown at the edge of the creek.

He aimed the rifle again at the overturned stage in time to see the head appear above the door opening. Mata Lobo's finger almost closed on the trigger, but he hesitated, seeing shoulders appear and then the rest of the body.

The man stopped uncertainly, looking around, cocking his ear to the silence. An odd-looking little man, fat and frightened, but not sure of what to be afraid. He clutched a small black case that singled him out as a drummer of some kind. He clutched it protectingly, shielding his means of existence.

When his gaze swept the hillside, perhaps he saw the glint of the rifle barrel, but if he did, it meant nothing to him. There was no reaction. And a second later it was too late. The .50-caliber bullet tore through his body to spin him off the coach.

Again silence settled. This time, longer. The wheels had stopped moving above the sprawled form of the guard.

Still Mata Lobo waited. His eyes, beneath the red calico headband, were nailed to the overturned Concord. He hadn't moved from his position. He sat stone still and waited. Watched and waited and counted.

He counted three dead: the driver, a passenger, and the guard who was in the road next to the coach—he was undoubtedly dead. But the run usually carried more passengers, at least two more, and that bothered the Apache.

Others might still be inside the coach, dead, wounded, or just waiting. Waiting with a cocked pistol. Either way Mata Lobo had to find out. He hadn't laid this ambush for sport alone. He needed bullets, and a shirt, and any glittering trinkets that might catch his eye. But it was the bullets, more than anything else, that finally made him raise himself and slip quietly down the side of the hill.

His Apache sense led him in a wide circle, so that when he approached the Concord, Banderas Creek was behind him. He walked half crouched, slowly, with short toe-to-heel strides, catlike, a coiled spring ready to snap. Mata Lobo was a Chiricahua Apache, well schooled in the ways of war.

He passed the baggage strewn about the ground without a side glance and dropped to his hands and knees as he came to the vertical wall that was the top of the coach. He touched the baggage rack lightly, then, pressing his ear against the smooth surface of the coach top, he remained fixed in this position for almost five minutes. Long, silent minutes.

He was about to rise, satisfied the coach was unoccupied, when he heard the sharp, scraping sound from within. Like someone moving a foot across a board.

He froze again, pressing close, then slowly placed his rifle on the ground beside him and lifted a skinning knife from a scabbard at his back.

He inched his body upward until he was standing, placed a foot on a rung of the baggage rack, and pushed his body up until his head was above the coach. He was confident of his own animal stealth. A gun could be waiting, but he doubted it. Only a fool would have moved, knowing he was just outside. A fool, or a child, or a woman.

Nor was he wrong. The woman was crouched against the roof of the coach, her back arched against the smooth surface, holding with both hands a long-barreled pistol that pointed toward the rear window. She was totally unaware of the Apache staring at her a few feet away, lying belly down on the side of the coach. When she saw him it was too late.

Revolver went up as knife came down, but the

knife was quicker and the heavy knob on the handle smashed against her knuckles to make her drop the revolver. Dark, vein-streaked arms reached in to drag her up through the door window. She struggled in his grasp, but only briefly, for he flung her from the coach and leapt down to the road after her.

She sat in the road dust and eyed him defiantly, her lips moving slightly, her eyes not wavering from his face. She screamed for the first time as she rose from the dust, but it was not a scream of fear.

She was almost to her feet when the Apache's hand tightened in her hair to fling her off balance back to the ground. He stood over her and looked down into the dust-streaked face. Then he turned back to the stagecoach.

She watched as he rummaged about the wreckage, sitting motionless, knowing that if she tried to run he would probably not hesitate to kill her. Her hands moved to her hair and unhurriedly brushed back the blond wisps that had been pulled from the tight chignon at the nape of her neck. Her hands moved slowly, almost unconsciously, and then down and in the same lifeless manner brushed the heavy dust from the green jersey traveling-dress, as if her movements were instinctive, not predetermined.

But her eyes were not lifeless. They followed the Apache's every move and narrowed slightly into two thin lines that contrasted sharply with her soft face, like fire on water. Her body moved from habit while her mind showed through her eyes.

She was afraid, but only loathing was on the surface. The fear was the stabbing weight in her breast, an emotion she had learned to control. She could have been in her late twenties, but her chin and the lines near her eyes told of at least six additional years.

Every now and then the Apache would glance back in her direction, but he found her always in the same position. She watched him bend over the still form of the guard lying on his back, and her eyes blinked hard as the Indian brought the stock of his rifle down on the man's forehead, but she did not turn her head.

There was no doubt now that all were dead. Mata Lobo was a thorough man, for his people had been slaying the *blanco* since the first war club smashed through the cumbersome armor of the conquistadors. His deeds were known throughout Apacheria; they whispered the name of the bronco Chiricahua with the bloodlust ever in his breast. There would be no survivor to tell of the lone Apache killer.

The sport of the affair had satisfied him, but he was angry. None of the men had been using a Sharps, so there was no ammunition to be had. He picked up the guard's Winchester, slinging the cartridge belt over his shoulder, but he liked the feel of the heavy buffalo rifle better. In the Sharps he had the confidence that comes only after trial. But he had only two cartridges left for it.

He turned his attention to the drummer, who was sprawled awkwardly next to the coach. With his foot he pushed the body over onto its back. A crimson smear spread over the shirtfront. The Apache opened the black satchel next to the man and emptied the contents onto the ground—needles, scissors, paring knives, and thread—and moved on to the horses.

His next act made the woman turn her head slightly, for with his skinning knife he sliced a large chunk of meat from the rump of a disabled horse and stuffed it into the sample case. Then he stepped to the front of the horse and cut the animal's jugular vein. Soon after, a Chiricahua Apache with a white woman at his side waded up Banderas Creek along the shallows. The woman dragged her legs through the water stiffly, slowly, as if her reluctance to move quickly was an open act of defiance toward the Indian.

The Chiricahua carried two rifles and a blood-stained satchel and wore a clean shirt, the tail hanging below his narrow hips. With every few steps his glance turned to the cold face of the woman. They disappeared three hundred yards upstream, where the creek cut a bend into the blackness of the pines.

★ ★ ★

It was the point riders of Phil Langmade's C Troop that found the wrecked stagecoach and the dead men, almost two hours later. Twenty days in the field and a brush with Nachee, and because of it they had missed the stage at Rindo's.

They were returning to the garrison at Inspiration, thighs aching from long, stiff hours in the saddle. Grimy, salt-sweat-white, alkali-caked—both their uniforms and their minds—after days of riding through the savage dust-glare of central Arizona. And of the forty mounts, three had ponchos draped over the saddles, bulging and shapeless. All patrols were not routine.

Langmade sent flankers to climb the ridges on both sides, and then went in. The troopers spread out in a semicircle, watching with hollow, lifeless eyes the flankers on the ridge more than the grisly scene on the road. You get used to the sight of death, but never to expecting it.

Langmade dismounted, but Simon Street, the civilian scout, rode up to the dead driver before throwing off. He walked upstream another hundred yards and then came back, approaching the officer from around the coach. The troopers sat still in their saddles, half-asleep, half-ready to throw up a carbine. Habit.

Langmade said, "I don't know if I want to find her inside the coach or not. If she's there, she's dead."

Street's eyes moved slowly over the scene. "You won't find her," he said. "There's a little heel print over on the bank. They went upstream. That's sure.

If they went down they'd wind up in the open near Rindo's."

Langmade boosted himself onto the side of the stage and came down almost in the same motion. He nodded his head to the scout and kept it moving in an arc along the top of the near ridge.

"Bet they laid up there waiting," Langmade said. "A month's pay they were Apaches."

Street followed his gaze to the ridge. He just glanced at the officer, his face creased-bronze and old beyond its years, crow's feet where eye met temple, his hat tilted low on his forehead, his eyes in shadow. "You're throwin' your money away, soldier," he said. "Apache."

Langmade looked at him quickly. "Only one?"

"That's all the sign says." Street pointed to the butchered horse. "A war party don't cut just one steak."

He turned his attention back to the ridge. He was looking at the exact spot from which the Apache had fired. Then his gaze fell slowly to sweep across the road to Banderas Creek. And he squinted against the glare as his eyes followed the course of the creek to the bend into the pines.

Langmade pushed his field hat back from his forehead, releasing the hot-steel grip of the sweatband, and watched the scout curiously. Langmade was young, in his mid-twenties, but he was good for a second lieutenant. He didn't talk much and he watched. He watched and he learned. And he knew he was learning from one of the best. But the tension was building inside his stomach, and it wasn't just the aftereffects of a twenty-day patrol.

There were three dead men in the road and a woman missing and it had happened because he had failed to bring the patrol in to Rindo's on time. The report would include an account of the brush with Nachee, and that would absolve him of blame. But it wouldn't make it easier for him to face Colonel Darck.

You didn't just look at a stone near your boot toe and say "sorry" to a man whose wife has been carried off by a blood-drunk Apache—even if you weren't to blame.

There it was. Langmade stood motionless, watching the scout. Langmade was in command, a commissioned officer in the United States Army, but he was tired. His bones ached and his mind dragged, weary of fighting the savage country and the elusive Apache who was a part of that country, and always there was so little time.

Learning to fight doesn't come easy with most men. Learning to fight the Apache doesn't come easy with anyone. You watch the veteran until your face takes on the same mask of impassiveness, then you make decisions.

He waited patiently for Street to say something, to give him a lead. He remembered forty troopers who watched the thin gold bars on his shoulders, and he tried to forget his helplessness.

Langmade said, "The colonel was coming from Thomas to meet Mrs. Darck at Inspiration." The scout was aware of this, he knew, but he had to say something. He had to fill the gap until something happened.

Simon Street looked at the officer and a half smile broke the thin line of his mouth. "We'll find her, soldier. It wasn't your fault. People get killed by Apaches every day."

As the words came out, he realized he had said the wrong thing and added, quickly, "Know who this looks like to me?" and then went on when Langmade looked but didn't speak.

"Looks like that bronco Apache we been chasin' on and off for five years. Nochalbestinay. Though the Mexicans named him Mata Lobo. He was a Turkey Creek Chiricahua who'd never get used to reservation life in seven hundred years. Sendin' him to San Carlos was like throwin' a mountain cat a hunk of raw meat and then pullin' all his teeth out."

Street pulled a thin cigar from his pocket and passed his tongue over the crumbling outer layer of tobacco. "You know, at one time there was almost a thousand troops plus a hundred Apache scouts all in the field at one time huntin' him, and no one even saw him. You couldn't ask the dead ones if they saw him or not. An Apache's bad enough, but this one's half devil."

He moved toward the butchered horse. "Boy's got a real yen for steak, ain't he?"

All the time the tension had been building in Langmade. Just standing there with his arms heavy at his sides and the weight pulling down inside his stomach. He had to hesitate until he was sure his voice would come out sounding natural.

"You've got the sign and I've got the men," he said. "Just point the way, Simon. Just point the way."

Street had turned and was walking toward his horse. He stopped and looked back at the officer. "Get your troop back to Inspiration and get a fresh patrol out, soldier."

Street's words were low, directed only to the officer, but Langmade raised his voice almost to a shout when he answered:

"We've got men here—get on his track!"

"I'm not goin' to guide for dead men," the scout answered easily. "If a thousand men can't catch him, you can't count on forty. Maybe just one's the answer. I don't want to tell you how to run your business, son, but if I was you I'd shake it back to Inspiration and get a fresh patrol out."

Street mounted and then looked down at Langmade, who had followed him over to the horse. "The trail's as fresh as you'd want it," he said, nodding toward the butchered horse. "That mare hasn't been dead three hours. And he's got a woman with him to slow him down."

"I've been out longer than that, Simon," Langmade said. "She'll slow him down just so long."

The scout's mouth turned slightly into a smile as he pressed his heels into the mare's flanks. "That's why I got to hurry, soldier."

He walked the mare toward Banderas Creek and kicked her into a gallop as he turned upstream.

* * *

AN HOUR BEFORE sunset Simon Street was walking his horse along the winding trail that threaded its way diagonally down the slope of the forest-covered hill that on the western side joined the rocky heights of the Sierra Apaches. This gradual leveling of the sierra was a tangled mass of junipers, gnarled stumps, and rock, rising and falling abruptly from one hillock to the next.

The trail gouged itself laboriously in a general southwesterly direction, fighting rock falls, pine, and prickly pear, finally to emerge miles to the south at Devil's Flats. From the crest, and occasionally down the path, you could see in the distance the whiteness—the bleak, bone-bleached whiteness—that was the flats.

Street had traveled a dozen-odd miles from the

ambush, making his way slowly at first along the creek bank, looking for a particular telltale sign. He knew the Apache had followed the creek, leaving no prints, but somewhere he had to come out.

The Apache would cover his tracks from the creek, but he would be coming out at a particular place for a reason. To pick up his mount. And you can't leave a horse tied in one place for any length of time without also leaving a sign. To recognize the place is something else.

Street saw the low tree branch that had been scarred by the hackamore, and his eyes fell to the particles of horse droppings that had remained after the Apache had swept most of it into the denser scrub brush. He was on the trail. From then on it was just a question of thinking like an Apache.

For the scout, that night, it was the last of his jerked beef and a quarter canteen of cold coffee. No fire. Cold, tasteless rations while he pressed his back against a smooth rock that was still warm from the day's heat and dueled his patience against the black pit that was the night.

His Winchester lay across his lap, and the slight pressure on his thighs was a feeling of reassurance against the loneliness of the night. Dead stillness, then the occasional night sound. He could be the only man in the world. Yet, just a few miles ahead, perhaps less, was a bronco Apache who would kill at the least provocation. And with him was a white woman.

Street rubbed the stock of the Winchester idly.

★ ★ ★

IN THE DUSK Amelia Darck watched the Apache. He crouched over the slab of red horsemeat, sitting on his heels, and hacked at the meat with his skinning knife. He cut off a chunk and stuffed it into his mouth, but the cold blood-taste of the raw meat tightened his throat muscles and he swallowed hard to get it down. He would wait.

He cut the slab of meat into thin strips and spread them out separately on a flat shelf of rock. When he had more time he would jerk the meat properly and have plenty to eat.

He looked toward the white woman and saw her staring at him. Always she stared, and always with the same fixed, strange look on her face. The eyes of the Apache and the white woman met, and Mata Lobo turned his attention back to the meat. The woman continued to stare at the Apache.

She sat on the ground with her arms extended behind her, full weight on her arms, propping her body in a rigid position, unmoving. Her legs extended straight out before her, the ankles lashed together with a strip of rawhide. And she continued to watch the Apache.

Amelia Darck saw an Apache for the first time when she was six years old. His face was vivid in her memory. She remembered once somebody had said, ". . . like glistening bacon rind." And always a dirty cloth headband.

Yuma, Whipple Barracks, Fort Apache, and Thomas. Officers' row on a sun-baked parade. Chiricahua, White Mountain, Mescalero, and Tonto. Thigh-high moccasins and a rusted Spencer. Tizwin drunk, then war drums. And only the red sun-slash in the sky after the patrol had faded into the glare three miles west of Thomas. Shapeless ponchos that used to be men. The old story. And she continued to watch the Apache.

Mata Lobo glanced at the woman, then stood up abruptly and walked toward her. He stooped at her feet, hesitated, then placed the blade of the knife between her ankles and jerked up with the blade, severing the rawhide string.

His face was expressionless, smooth and impassive, as he eased his body to the ground. A face that in the dimness was shadow on stone. His hands pushed against her shoulders until her arms bent slowly and her back was flat against the short, sparse grass.

The hands moved from her shoulder and touched her face gently, the fingers moving on her cheeks like a blind man's identifying an object, and his body eased toward hers.

Her face was the same. The eyes open, infrequently blinking. She smelled the sour dirt-smell of the Apache's body. Then she opened her arms and pulled him to her.

★ ★ ★

SIMON STREET was up before dawn. He gave his tightening stomach the last of the cold, stale coffee while he waited for the sun to peel back another layer of the morning darkness. It was cold and damp for that time of the year, and when he again started down the trail, a gray mist hung from the lower branches of the trees and lay softly against the grotesque rock lines.

More often now, the ground fell away to the left, the trail hugging the side of the hill in its diagonal descent; and in the distance was a sheet of milky smoke where the mist clung softly to the flats. The trail was narrow and rocky and lined with dense brush most of the way down.

Less than a mile ahead the grade dropped again steeply to the left of the trail, bare of tree or rock, cutting a smooth swatch twenty yards wide through the pines. The mist had evaporated considerably by then and Street could see almost to the bottom of the slide.

First, it was the faintest blur of motion. And then the sound. A sound that could be human.

Simon Street had been riding half tensed for the past dozen years. There was no abrupt stop. He reined in gently with a soothing murmur into the mare's ear, and slid from the saddle, whispering again to the mare as he tied the reins to a pine branch a foot from the ground.

He made his way along the trail until the slope was again thick with brush and trees, and there he began his descent. A yard at a time, making sure of firm ground before each step, bending branches slowly so there would be no warning swish. And every few yards he would hug the ground and wait, swinging his gaze in every direction, even behind.

He had gone almost a hundred yards when he saw the woman.

He crouched low to the sandy ground and crawled under the full branches of a pine, watching the woman almost thirty yards away. She was sitting on something just off the ground, her back resting against the smoothness of a birch tree.

He was approaching her from the rear and could see only part of her head and shoulder resting against the tree trunk. The brush near her cut off the lower part of her body, but there was something strange about her position—her immobility, the way her shoulder was thrown back so tightly against the roundness of the birch. Street had the feeling she was dead. Time would tell.

He lay motionless under the thick foliage and waited, the Winchester in front of him. And Simon Street had his thoughts. You never get used to the sight of a white woman after an Apache has finished with her. An hour later, a week later, a dozen years later, the picture will flash in your memory, vivid, stark naked of hazy forgetfulness.

And the form of the Apache will be there, too, close like the smothering reek of a hot animal, though you may have never seen him. Then you will be sick if you are the kind. Street wasn't the kind, but he didn't look forward to approaching the woman.

After almost a half hour he again began to work his way toward the woman. In that length of time he had not moved. Nor had the woman. If she was dead, the Apache would probably be gone. But that was guessing, and when you guess, you take a chance.

He crawled all the way, slowly, a foot at a time, until he was directly behind the birch. Then he reached up, his hand sliding along the white bark, and touched her shoulder lightly.

Amelia Darck jumped to her feet and turned in the motion. Her face was powder white, her eyes wide, startled; but when she saw the scout the color seemed to creep through her cheeks and her mouth broke into a fragile smile.

"You're late, Mr. Street. I've waited a good many hours."

The scout was momentarily stunned. He knew his face bore a foolish expression, but there was nothing he could do about it.

The woman's face regained its composure quickly and once again she was the colonel's lady. Though there was a drawn look and a darker shadow about the eyes that could not be wiped away with a polite smile.

Then Street saw the Apache. He was lying belly down in the short grass, close behind Mrs. Darck. Street took a step to her side and saw the handle of the skinning knife sticking straight up from the Apache's back. The cotton shirt was deep crimson in a wide smear around the knife handle.

He looked at her again with the foolish look still on his face.

"Mr. Street, I've been sitting up all night with a dead Indian and I'm almost past patience. Would you kindly take me to my husband."

He looked again at the Apache and then to the woman. Disbelief in his eyes. He started to say something, but Amelia Darck went on.

"I've lived out here most of my life, Mr. Street, as you know. I heard Apache war drums long before I attended my first cotillion, but I have hardly reached the point where I have to take an Apache for a lover."

Simon Street saw a thousand troops and a hundred scouts in the field. Then he looked at the slender woman walking briskly up the grade.

4

The Rustlers

MOST OF THE time there was dead silence. When someone did say something it was never more than a word or two at a time: *More coffee?* Words that were not words because there was no thought behind them and they didn't mean anything. Words like *getting late,* when no one cared. Hardly even noises, because no one heard.

Stillness. Six men sitting together in a pine grove, and yet there was no sound. A boot scraped gravel and a tin cup clanked against rock, but they were like the words, little noises that started and stopped at the same time and were forgotten before they could be remembered.

More coffee? And an answering grunt that meant even less.

Five men scattered around a campfire that was dead, and the sixth man squatting at the edge of the pines looking out into the distance through the dismal reflection of a dying sun that made the grayish flat land look petrified in death and unchanged for a hundred million years.

Emmett Ryan stared across the flats toward the lighter gray outline in the distance that was Anton Chico, but he wasn't seeing the adobe brick of the village. He wasn't watching the black speck that was gradually getting bigger as it approached.

All of us knew that. We sat and watched Emmett Ryan's coat pulled tight across his shoulder blades, not moving body or head. Just a broad smoothness of faded denim. We'd been looking at the same back all the way from Tascosa and in two hundred miles you can learn a lot about a back.

The black speck grew into a horse and rider, and as they moved up the slope toward the pines the horse and rider became Gosh Hall on his roan. Emmett walked over to meet him, but didn't say anything. The question was on his broad, red face and he didn't have to ask it.

Gosh Hall swung down from the saddle and put his hands on the small of his back, arching against the stiffness. "They just rode in," he said, and walked past the big man to the dead fire. "Who's got all the coffee?"

Emmett followed him with his eyes and the question was still there. It was something to see that big, plain face with the eyes open wide and staring when before they'd always been half-closed from squinting against the glare of twenty-odd years in open country. Now his face looked too big and loose for the small nose and slit of an Irish mouth. You could see the indecision and maybe a little fear in the wide-open eyes, something that had never been there before.

We'd catch ourselves looking at that face and have to look at something else, quick, or Em would see somebody's jaw hanging open and wonder what the hell was wrong with him. We felt sorry for Em—I know I did—and it was a funny feeling to all of a sudden see the big TX ramrod that way.

Gosh looked like he had an apron on, standing over the dead fire with his hip cocked and the worn hide chaps covering his short legs. He held the cup halfway to his face, watching Em, waiting for him to ask the question. I thought Gosh was making it a little extra tough on Em; he could have come right out with it. Both of them just stared at each other.

Finally Emmett said, "Jack with them?"

Gosh took a sip of coffee first. "Him and Joe Anthony rode in together, and another man. Anthony and the other man went into the Senate House and Jack took the horses to the livery and then followed them over to the hotel."

"They see you?"

"Naw, I was down the street under a ramada. All they'd see'd be shadow."

"You sure it was them, Gosh?" I asked him.

"Charlie," Gosh said, "I got a picture in my head, and it's stuck there 'cause I never expected to see one like it. It's a picture of Jack and Joe Anthony riding into Magenta the same way a month ago. When you see something that's different or hadn't ought to be, it sticks in your head. And they was on the same mounts, Charlie."

Emmett went over to his dun mare and tightened the cinch like he wanted to keep busy and show us everything was going the same. But he was just fumbling with the strap, you could see that. His head swung around a few inches. "Jack look all right?"

Gosh turned his cup upside down and a few drops of coffee trickled down to the ashes at his feet. "I don't know, Em. How is a man who's just stole a hundred head of beef supposed to look?"

Emmett jerked his body around and the face was closed again for the first time in a week, tight and redder than usual. Then his jaw eased and his big hands hanging at his sides opened and closed and then went loose. Emmett didn't have anything to grab. Some of the others were looking at Gosh Hall and probably wondering why the little rider was making it so hard for Em.

Emmett asked him, "Did you see Butzy?"

"He didn't ride in. I 'magine he's out with the herd." Gosh looked around. "Neal still out, huh?"

Neal Whaley had gone in earlier with Gosh, then split off over to where they were holding the herd, just north of Anton Chico. Neal was to watch and tell us if they moved them. Emmett figured they were holding the herd until a buyer came along. There were a lot of buyers in New Mexico who didn't particularly care what the brand read, but Emmett said they were waiting for a top bid or they would have sold all the stock before this.

Ned Bristol and Lloyd Cohane got up and stretched and then just stood there awkwardly looking at the dead fire, their boots, and each other. Lloyd pulled a blue bandanna from his coat pocket and wiped his face with it, then folded it and straightened it out thin between his fingers before tilting his chin up to tie it around his neck. Ned pushed his gun belt down lower on his hips and watched Emmett.

Dobie Shaw, the kid in our outfit, went over to his mount and pulled his Winchester from the boot and felt in the bag behind the saddle for a box of cartridges. Dobie had to do something too.

Ben Templin was older; he'd been riding better

than thirty years. He eased back to the ground with his hands behind his head tilting his hat over his face and waited. Ben had all the time in the world.

Everybody was going through the motions of being natural, but fidgeting and acting restless and watching Emmett at the same time because we all knew it was time now, and Emmett didn't have any choice. That was what forced Emmett's hand, though we knew he would have done it anyway, sooner or later. But maybe we looked a little too anxious to him, when it was only restlessness. It was a long ride from Tascosa. A case of let's get it over with or else go on home—one way or the other, regardless of whose brother stole the cows.

Gosh Hall scratched the toe of his boot through the sand, kicking it over the ashes of the dead fire. "About that time, ain't it, Em?"

Emmett exhaled like he was very tired. "Yeah, it's about that time." He looked at every face, slowly, before turning to his mare.

★ ★ ★

IT'S ROUGHLY a hundred and thirty miles from Tascosa, following the Canadian, to Trementina on the Conchas, then another thirty-five miles south, swinging around Mesa Montosa to Anton Chico, on the Pecos. Counting detours to find water holes and trailing the wrong sign occasionally, that's about two hundred miles of sun, wind, and New

Mexico desert—and all to bring back a hundred head of beef owned by a Chicago company that tallied close to a quarter million all over the Panhandle and north-central Texas.

The western section of the TX Company was headquartered at Sudan that year, with most of the herds north of Tascosa and strung out west along the Canadian. Emmett Ryan was ramrod of the home crew at Sudan, but he spent a week or more at a time out on the grass with the herds. That was why he happened to be with us when R. D. Perris, the company man, rode in. We were readying to go into Magenta for a few when Perris came beating his mount into camp. Even in the cool of the evening the horse was flaked white and about to drop and Perris was so excited he could hardly get the words out. And finally when he told his story there was dead silence and all you could hear was R. D. Perris breathing like his chest was about to rip open.

Jack Ryan and Frank Butzinger—Frank, who nobody ever gave credit for having any sand—and over a hundred head of beef hadn't been seen on the west range for three days. R. D. Perris had said, "The tracks follow the river west, but we figured Jack was taking them to new grass. But then the tracks just kept on going. . . ."

Emmett was silent from that time on. He asked a few questions, but he was pretty sure of the answers before he asked them. There was that talk for weeks about Jack having been seen in Tascosa and Magenta with Joe Anthony. And there weren't many people friendly with Joe Anthony. In his time, he'd had his picture on wanted dodgers more than once. Two shootings for sure, and a few holdups, but the holdups were just talk. Nobody ever pinned anything on him, and with his gunhand reputation, nobody made any accusations.

Gosh Hall had seen them together in Magenta and he told Emmett to his face that he didn't like it; but Emmett had defended him and said Jack was just sowing oats because he was still young and hadn't got his sense of values yet. But Lloyd Cohane was there that time at the line camp when Emmett dropped in and chewed hell out of Jack for palling with Joe Anthony. Then came the time Emmett walked into the saloon in Tascosa with his gun out and pushed it into Joe Anthony's belly before Joe even saw him and told him to ride and keep riding.

Jack was there, drunk like he usually was in town, but he sobered quick and followed Anthony out of the saloon when Emmett prodded him out, and laughed right in Emmett's face when Em told him to stay where he was. And he was laughing and weaving in the saddle when he rode out of town with Anthony.

Until that night Perris came riding in with his

story, Em hadn't seen his brother. So you know what he was thinking; what all of us were thinking.

Riding the two hundred miles to find the herd was part of the job, but knowing you were trailing a friend made the job kind of sour and none of us was sure if we wanted to find the cattle. Jack Ryan was young and wild and drank too much and laughed all the time, but he had more friends than any rider in the Panhandle.

Like Ben Templin said: "Jack's a good boy, but he's got an idea life's just a big can-can dancer with four fingers of scootawaboo in each hand." And that was about it.

★ ★ ★

THE SPLOTCH of white that was Anton Chico from a distance gradually got bigger and cleared until finally right in front of us it was gray adobe brick, blocks of it, dull and lifeless in the cold late sunlight. Emmett slowed us to a walk the last few hundred feet approaching the town's main street and motioned Ben Templin up next to him.

"Ben," he said, "you take Dobie with you and cut for that back street yonder and come up behind the livery. Don't let anybody see you and hush the stableman if he gets loud about what you're doing. Maybe Butzy'll come along, Ben—if he isn't there already."

I looked at Emmett watching Ben Templin and Dobie Shaw cut off, and there it was. His old face again. All closed and hard with the crow's feet streaking from the corners of his eyes. And his mouth tight like it used to be when he thought and ordered men at the same time, because he always knew what he was doing. You could see Emmett knew what he was doing now, that he'd set his mind. And when Emmett Ryan set his mind his pride saw to it that it stayed set.

Emmett walked his mount down the left side of the narrow main street with the rest of us strung out behind. When he veered over to a hitchrack about halfway down the second block, we veered with him and tied up, straggled along before two store fronts.

Em stepped up on the boardwalk and moved leisurely toward the Senate House hotel almost at the end of the block. He stopped as he crossed the alley next to the hotel and nodded to Lloyd Cohane, then bent his head toward the alley and moved it in a half-circle over his big shoulders. Lloyd moved off down the alley toward the back of the hotel.

"Go on with him, Ned," Em whispered. "Stick near the kitchen door and if anybody but the cook comes out shoot his pants off."

Ned moved off after Lloyd, both carrying carbines. Em looked at Gosh and me, but didn't say anything. He just looked and that meant we were with him and supposed to back up anything he did. Then he turned toward the hotel and slipped his revolver out in the motion. Gosh moved right after him and pointed the barrel of his Winchester out in front of him.

Two idlers sitting in front of the hotel stared at us trying to make out they weren't staring, and as soon as we passed them I heard their chairs scrape and their footsteps hurrying down the boards. A man across the street pushed through the saloon doors without even putting his hands out. A rider slowed up in front of the hotel as if about to turn in and then he kicked his mount into a trot down the street.

In the hotel lobby you could still hear the horse clopping down the street and it made the lobby seem even more quiet and comfortable, feeling the coolness inside and picturing the horse on the dusty street. But there was the clerk with his mouth open watching Emmett walk toward the café entrance, his spurs chinging with each step.

It seemed like, for a show like this, everything was moving too fast. The next thing, we were in the café part and Jack Ryan and Joe Anthony and the other man were looking at us like they couldn't believe their eyes.

None of them moved. Jack's jaw was open with a mouthful of beef, his eyes almost as wide open as his mouth. The other man had a taco in his fingers raised halfway to his mouth and he just held it there. Didn't move it up or down. Joe Anthony's right hand was around a glass of something yellow like mescal. His left hand was below the level of the table. The three of them had their hats on, pushed back, and they looked dirty and tired.

Jack chewed and swallowed hard and then he smiled. "Damn, Em, you must have flown!"

The other man looked at us one at a time slowly, then shrugged his shoulders and said, "What the hell," and shoved the taco in his mouth.

Joe Anthony wiped the back of his hand over his mouth and moved the hand back, smoothing the long mustaches with the knuckle of his index finger. The other hand was still under the table.

Emmett held his revolver pointed square at Joe Anthony and seemed to be unmindful of the other two men. Lloyd and Ned came through the kitchen door and moved around behind Emmett.

"Get up," Em ordered. "And take off your belts."

Somebody's chair scraped, but Joe Anthony said, "Hold it!" and it was quiet.

Anthony was staring back at Emmett. "Do I look like a green kid to you, Ryan?" he said, and half smiled. "You're not telling anybody what to do, cowboy."

"I said get up," Em repeated.

Joe Anthony kept on smiling like he thought Emmett was a fool. He shook his head slowly. "Ryan, the longer you stand there, the shorter your chances are of leaving here on your two feet."

"You're all mouth," Emmett said. "Just mouth."

The outlaw's expression didn't change. His face was good-looking in a swarthy kind of way, but gaunt and hungry-looking with pale, shallow eyes like a man who forgot where his conscience was, or that he ever had one.

His smile sagged a little and he said, "Ryan, let's quit playing. You ride the hell out of here before I shoot you."

"I'm not playing," Emmett said, leveling the revolver. "Get up, quick."

"Ryan," Joe Anthony whispered impatiently, "I've had a Colt leveled on your belly since the second you come through that doorway."

I thought I knew Emmett Ryan, but I didn't know him as well as I supposed. His face didn't change its expression, but his finger moved on the trigger and the room filled with the explosion. His thumb yanked on the hammer and he fired again right on top of the first one.

Joe Anthony went back with his chair, fell hard and lay still. His pistol was still in the holster on his right hip.

Emmett looked down at him. "You're all mouth, Anthony. All mouth."

Nobody said anything after that. We were looking at Em and Em was looking at Joe Anthony stretched out on the floor. I heard steps behind me and there was Dobie Shaw tiptoeing in and looking like he'd dive out the window if anybody said anything.

Emmett waved his gun at the other man and glanced at his brother. "Who's this?"

Jack spoke easily. "Earl Roach. We picked him up for a trail driver. He didn't know it was rustled stock."

Roach was unfastening his gun belt. He shot a look toward Jack. "Boy," he said, "you take care of your troubles and I'll take care of mine."

Dobie Shaw moved up behind Emmett hesitantly and waited for the big foreman to look his way. "Mr. Ryan—Ben's holding Butzy over to the livery." He went on hurriedly trying to get the whole story out before Em asked any questions. "Butzy walked right in and didn't move after Ben throwed down on him, but there was another one back a ways and he turned and rode like hell when he saw me and Ben with our guns out. Me and Ben didn't even get a shot at him 'fore he was round the corner and gone."

"All right, Dobie. You go on back with Ben." Emmett hesitated and glanced at Jack like he was making up his mind all over again, but the doubt passed off quickly. He said, "We'll be over directly. You go on and tell Ben to keep Butzy right there."

* * *

FRANK BUTZINGER was flat against the boards of a stall, though Ben Templin was standing across the open part of the stable smoking a cigarette with his carbine propped against the wall. Ben wasn't paying any attention to him, but even in the dim light you could see Butzy was about ready to die of fright.

Gosh Hall pushed Jack and Earl Roach toward the stall that Butzy was in and mumbled something, probably swearing. Jack looked around at him with a half smile and shook his head like a father playing Indians with his youngster. Humoring him.

Emmett stood out in the open part with the rest of us spread around now. He said, "You sell the stock yet?"

"A few," Jack answered. "We got almost a hundred head."

"You got the money?"

"What do you think?"

The foreman motioned to Gosh Hall. "Get some line and tie their hands behind them."

The little cowboy's face brightened and he moved into the stall lifting a coil of rope from the side wall. When he pulled his knife and started to cut it into pieces, the stableman came running over. He'd been standing in the front doorway, but I hadn't noticed him there before.

He ran over yelling, "Hey, that's my rope!"

Gosh reached out, laughing, and grabbed one of his braces and snapped it against his faded red-flannel undershirt. "Get back, old man, you're interfering with justice." Then he pushed the man hard against the stall partition.

Emmett took hold of his elbow and pulled him out toward the front of the livery. "You stay out here," he said. "This isn't any of your business." He turned from the man and nodded his head to the stalls where three horses were.

The stable was large, high-ceilinged, with stalls lining both sides. The open area was wide, but longer than it was wide, with heavy timbers overhead reaching from lofts on both sides that ran the length of the stable above the stalls. The stable was empty but for the three horses toward the back.

"Bring those horses up here." Em said it to no one in particular.

When Dobie and Ned and I led the mounts up, I heard Lloyd ask Em if he should go get our horses. Em shook his head, but didn't say anything.

Lloyd said, "Shouldn't we be getting out to the stock, Em?"

"We got time. Neal's watching the cows," Em reminded him. "The man that was with Butzy spread his holler if there were any others out there. They'd be halfway to Santa Fe by now."

He turned on Gosh impatiently. "Come on, get 'em mounted."

I picked up one of their saddles from the rack and walked up behind Gosh, who was pushing the three men toward the horses.

"Look out, Gosh. Let me get the saddles on before you get in the way. You can't throw 'em on with your arms behind your back."

Gosh twisted his mouth into a smile and looked past me at Emmett. There was a wad of tobacco in his cheek that made his thin face lopsided, like a jagged rock with hair on it. He shifted the wad, still smiling, and then spit over to the side.

"You tell him, Em," he said.

Emmett looked at me with his closed-up, leathery face. He stared hard as if afraid his eyes would waver. "They don't need the saddles."

Gosh swatted me playfully with the end of rope in his hand. "Want me to paint you a picture, Charlie?" He laughed and walked out through the wide entrance.

Gosh didn't have to paint a picture. Ben Templin dropped his cigarette. Lloyd and Ned and Dobie just stared at Emmett, but none of them said anything. Em stood there like a rock and stared back like he was defying anybody to object.

The boys looked away and moved about uncomfortably. They weren't about to go against Emmett Ryan. They were used to doing what they were told because Em was always right, and weren't sure that he wasn't right even now. A hanging isn't an uncommon thing where there is little law. Along the Pecos there was less than little. Still, it didn't rub right—even if Em was following his conscience, it didn't rub right.

I hesitated until the words were in my mouth and I'd have had bit my tongue off to hold them back. "You setting yourself up as the law?" It was supposed to have a bite to it, but the words sounded weak and my voice wasn't even.

Emmett said, "You know what the law is." He beckoned to the coil of rope Gosh had hung back on the boards. "That's it right there, Charlie. You know better than that." Emmett was talking to himself as well as me, but you didn't remind that hardheaded Irishman of things like that.

"Look, Em. Let's get the law and handle this right."

"It's black and white, it's two and two, if you steal cows and get caught you hang."

"Maybe. But it's not up to you to decide. Let's get the law."

"I've already decided," was all he said.

The stable hand crept up close to us and waited until there was a pause. "The deputy ain't here," the old man said. "He rode down to Lincoln yesterday morning to join the posse." He waited for someone to show interest, but no one said a word. "They're getting a posse up on account of there's word Bill Bonney's at Fort Sumner."

He stepped back looking proud as could be over his news. I could have kicked his seat flat for what he said.

Gosh came back with two coiled lariats on his arm and a third one in his hands. He was shaping a knot at one end of it.

Earl Roach looked at Gosh, then up to the heavy rafter that crossed above the three horses, then Jack's head went up too.

Gosh spit and grinned at them, forming a loop in the second rope. "What'd you expect'd happen?"

Jack kept his eyes on the rafter. "I didn't expect to get caught."

"Jack's always smiling into the sunshine, ain't he?" Gosh pushed Earl Roach toward his horse. "Mount up, mister."

Roach jerked his shoulder away from him. "I look like a bird to you? You want me up on that horse, you'll have to put me up."

"Earl, I'll put you up and help take you down."

When he got to Butzy and offered him a leg up, Butzy made a funny sound like a whine and started to back away, but Gosh grabbed him by his shirt before he took two steps. Butzy looked over Gosh's bony shoulder, his eyes popping out of his pasty face.

"Em, what you fixin' to do?" His voice went up a notch, and louder. "What you fixin' to do? You just scarin' us, Em?"

If it was a joke, Butzy didn't want to play the fool, but you could tell by his voice what he was thinking. Em didn't answer him.

Gosh finished knotting the third rope and handed it to Dobie, who looked at it like he'd never seen a lariat before.

Gosh said, "Make yourself useful and throw that rope over the rafter."

He went out and brought his horse in and mounted so he could slip the nooses over their heads, but he stood in the stirrups and still couldn't reach the tops of their heads. Emmett told him to get down and ordered Ben Templin to climb up and fix the ropes. Ben did it, but Em had to tell him three times.

Before he jumped down, Ben lighted cigarettes and gave them to Jack and Earl. Butzy was weaving his head around so Ben couldn't get one in his mouth. Just rolling his head around with his eyes closed, moaning.

Gosh looked up at him and laughed out loud. "You praying, Butzy?" he called out. "Better pray hard, you ain't got much time," and kept on laughing.

Ben Templin made a move toward Gosh, but Emmett caught his arm.

"Hold still, Ben." He looked past him at Gosh. "You can do what you're doing with your mouth shut."

Gosh moved behind the horses with the short end of rope in his hand. He edged over behind Earl Roach's horse. "Age before beauty, I always say."

Butzy's eyes opened up wide. "God, Em! Please Em—please—honest to God—I didn't know they was stealing the herd! Swear to God, Em, I thought Perris told Jack to sell the herd. Please, Em—I—let me go and I'll never show my face again. Please—"

"You'll never show it anyway where you're going," Gosh cracked.

Earl Roach was looking at Butzy with a blank expression. His head turned to Jack, holding his chin up to ease his neck away from the chafe of the rope. "Who's your friend?"

Jack Ryan's lips, with the cigarette hanging, formed a small smile at Roach. "Never saw him before in my life." His young face was paler than usual, you could see it through beard and sunburn, but his voice was slow and even with that little edge of sarcasm it usually carried.

Roach shook his head to drop the ash from his cigarette. "Beats me where he come from," he said.

Ben Templin swore in a slow whisper. He mumbled, "It's a damn waste of good guts."

Lloyd and Ned and Dobie were looking at the

two of them like they couldn't believe their eyes and then seemed to all drop their heads about the same time. Embarrassed. Like they didn't rate to be in the same room with Jack and Earl. I felt it too, but felt a mad coming on along with it.

"Dammit, Em! You're going to wait for the deputy!" I knew I was talking, but it didn't sound like me. "You're going to wait for the deputy whether you like it or not!"

Emmett just stared back and I felt like running for the door. Emmett stood there alone like a rock you couldn't budge and then Ben Templin was beside him with his hand on Em's arm, but not just resting it there, holding the forearm hard. His other hand was on his pistol butt.

"Charlie's right, Em," Ben said. "I'm not sure how you got us this far, or why, but ain't you or God Almighty going to hang those boys by yourself."

They stood there, those two big men, their faces not a foot apart, not telling a thing by their faces, but you got the feeling if one of them moved the livery would collapse like a twister hit it.

Finally Emmett blinked his eyes, and moved his arm to make Ben let go.

"All right, Ben." It was just above a whisper and sounded tired. "We've all worked together a long time and have always agreed—if it was a case of letting you in on the agreeing. We won't change it now."

Gosh came out from behind the horses. Disappointed and mad. He moved right up close to Emmett. "You going to let this woman—"

That was all he got a chance to say. Emmett swung his fist against that bony tobacco bulge and Gosh flattened against the board wall before sliding down into a heap.

Emmett started to walk out the front and then he turned around. "We're waiting on the deputy until tomorrow morning. If he don't show by then, this party takes up where it left off."

He angled out the door toward the Senate House, still the boss. The hardheaded Irishman's pride had to get the last word in whether he meant it or not.

★ ★ ★

THE DEPUTY got back late that night. You could see by his face that he hadn't gotten what he'd gone for. Emmett stayed in his room at the Senate House, but Ben Templin and I were waiting at the jail when the deputy returned—though I don't know what we would have done if he hadn't—with two bottles of the yellowest mescal you ever saw to ease his saddle sores and dusty throat.

We told him how we'd put three of our boys in his jail—just a scare, you understand—when they'd got drunk and thought it'd be fun to run off with a few head of stock. Just a joke on the owner, you understand. And Emmett Ryan, the ramrod, being one of them's brother, he had to act tougher than usual, else the boys'd think he was playing favorites. Like him always giving poor Jack the wildest broncs and making him ride drag on the trail drives.

Em was always a little too serious, anyway. Of course, he was a good man, but he was a big, red-faced Irishman who thought his pride was a stone god to burn incense in front of. And hell, he had enough troubles bossing the TX crew without getting all worked up over his brother getting drunk and playing a little joke on the owners—you been drunk like that, haven't you, Sheriff? Hell, everybody has. A sheriff with guts enough to work in Bill Bonney's country had more to do than chase after drunk cowpokes who wouldn't harm a fly. And even if they were serious, what's a few cows to an outfit that owns a quarter million?

And along about halfway down the second bottle— So why don't we turn the joke around on old Em and let the boys out tonight? We done you a turn by getting rid of Joe Anthony. Old Em'll wake up in the morning and be madder than hell when he finds out, and that will be some sight to see.

The deputy could hardly wait.

In the morning it was Ben who had to tell Em what happened. I was there in body only, with my head pounding like a pulverizer. The deputy didn't show up at all.

We waited for Emmett to fly into somebody, but he just looked at us, from one to the next. Finally he turned toward the livery.

"Let's go take the cows home," was all he said.

Not an hour later we were looking down at the flats along the Pecos where the herd was. Neal Whaley was riding toward us.

Emmett had been riding next to me all the way out from Anton Chico. When he saw Neal, he broke into a gallop to meet him, and that was when I thought he said, "Thanks, Charlie."

I know his head turned, but there was the beat of his horse when he started the gallop, and that mescal pounding at my brains. Maybe he said it and maybe he didn't.

Knowing that Irishman, I'm not going to ask him.

5

The Big Hunt

It was a Sharps .50, heavy and cumbrous, but he was lying at full length downwind of the herd behind the rise with the long barrel resting on the hump of the crest so that the gun would be less tiring to fire.

He counted close to fifty buffalo scattered over the grass patches, and his front sight roamed over the herd as he waited. A bull, its fresh winter hide glossy in the morning sun, strayed leisurely from the others, following thick patches of gamma grass. The Sharps swung slowly after the animal. And when the bull moved directly toward the rise, the heavy rifle dipped over the crest so that the sight was just off the right shoulder. The young man, who was still not much more than a boy, studied the animal with mounting excitement.

"Come on, granddaddy . . . a little closer," Will Gordon whispered. The rifle stock felt comfortable against his cheek, and even the strong smell of oiled metal was good. "Walk up and take it like a man, you ugly monster, you dumb, shaggy, ugly hulk of a monster. Look at that fresh gamma right in front of you. . . ."

The massive head came up sleepily, as if it had heard the hunter, and the bull moved toward the rise. It was less than eighty yards away, nosing the grass tufts, when the Sharps thudded heavily in the crisp morning air.

The herd lifted from grazing, shaggy heads turning lazily toward the bull sagging to its knees, but as it slumped to the ground the heads lowered unconcernedly. Only a few of the buffalo paused to sniff the breeze. A calf bawled, sounding *nooooo* in the open-plain stillness.

Will Gordon had reloaded the Sharps, and he pushed it out in front of him as another buffalo lumbered over to the fallen bull, sniffing at the blood, nuzzling the bloodstained hide: and, when the head came up, nose quivering with scent, the boy squeezed the trigger. The animal stumbled a few yards before easing its great weight to the ground.

Don't let them smell blood, he said to himself. They smell blood and they're gone.

He fired six rounds then, reloading the Sharps each time, though a loaded Remington rolling-block lay next to him. He fired with little hesitation, going to his side, ejecting, taking a cartridge from the loose pile at his elbow, inserting it in the open breech. He fired without squinting, calmly, killing a buffalo with each shot. Two of the animals lumbered on a short distance after being hit, glassy eyed, stunned by the shock of the heavy bullet. The others dropped to the earth where they stood.

Sitting up now, he pulled a square of cloth from his coat pocket, opened his canteen, and poured water into the cloth, squeezing it so that it would become saturated. He worked the wet cloth through the eye of his cleaning rod, then inserted it slowly into the barrel of the Sharps, hearing a sizzle as it passed through the hot metal tube. He was new to the buffalo fields, but he had learned how an overheated gun barrel could put a man out of business. He had made sure of many things before leaving Leverette with just a two-man outfit.

Pulling the rod from the barrel, he watched an old cow sniffing at one of the fallen bulls. Get that one quick . . . or you'll lose a herd!

He dropped the Sharps, took the Remington, and fired at the buffalo from a sitting position. Then he reloaded both rifles, but fired the Remington a half-dozen more rounds while the Sharps cooled. Twice he had to hit with another shot to kill, and he told himself to take more time. Perspiration beaded his face, even in the crisp fall air, and burned powder was heavy in his nostrils, but he kept firing at the same methodical pace, because it could not last much longer, and there was not time to cool the barrels properly. He had killed close to twenty when the blood smell became too strong.

The buffalo made rumbling noises in the thickness of their throats, and now three and four at a time would crowd toward those on the ground, sniffing, pawing nervously.

A bull bellowed, and the boy fired again. The herd bunched, bumping each other, bellowing, shaking their clumsy heads at the blood smell. Then the leader broke suddenly, and what was left of the herd was off, from stand to dead run, in one moment of panic, driven mad by the scent of death.

The boy fired into the dust cloud that rose behind them, but they were out of range before he could reload again.

It's better to wave them off carefully with a blanket after killing all you can skin, the boy thought to himself. But this had worked out all right. Sometimes it didn't, though. Sometimes they stampeded right at the hunter.

He rose stiffly, rubbing his shoulder, and moved back down the rise to his picketed horse. His shoulder ached from the buck of the heavy rifles, but he felt good. Lying back there on the plain was close to seventy or eighty dollars he'd split with Leo Cleary . . . soon as they'd been skinned and handed over to the hide buyers. Hell, this was easy. He lifted his hat, and the wind was cold on his sweat-dampened forehead. He breathed in the air, feeling an exhilaration, and the ache in his shoulder didn't matter one bit.

Wait until he rode into Leverette with a wagon full of hides, he thought. He'd watch close, pretending he didn't care, and he'd see if anybody laughed at him then.

★ ★ ★

HE WAS MOUNTING when he heard the wagon creaking in the distance, and he smiled when Leo Cleary's voice drifted up the gradual rise, swearing at the team. He waited in the saddle, and swung down as the four horses and the canvas-topped wagon came up to him.

"Leo, I didn't even have to come wake you up." Will Gordon smiled up at the old man on the box, and the smile eased the tight lines of his face. It was a face that seemed used to frowning, watching life turn out all wrong, a sensitive boyish face, but the set of his jaw was a man's . . . or that of a boy who thought like a man. There were few people he showed his smile to other than Leo Cleary.

"That cheap store whiskey you brought run out," Leo Cleary said. His face was beard stubbled, and the skin hung loosely seamed beneath tired eyes.

"I thought you quit," the boy said. His smile faded.

"I have now."

"Leo, we got us a lot of money lying over that rise."

"And a lot of work. . . ." He looked back into the wagon, yawning. "We got near a full load we could take in . . . and rest up. You shooters think all the work's in knocking 'em down."

"Don't I help with the skinning?"

Cleary's weathered face wrinkled into a slow smile. "That's just the old man in me coming out," he said. "You set the pace, Will. All I hope is roaming hide buyers don't come along . . . you'll be wanting to stay out till April." He shook his head. "That's a mountain of back-breaking hours just to prove a point."

"You think it's worth it or not?" the boy said angrily.

Cleary just smiled. "Your dad would have liked to seen this," he said. "Come on, let's get those hides."

Skinning buffalo was filthy, back-straining work. Most hunters wouldn't stoop to it. It was for men hired as skinners and cooks, men who stayed by the wagons until the shooting was done.

During their four weeks on the range the boy did his share of the work, and now he and Leo Cleary went about it with little conversation. Will Gordon was not above helping with the butchering, with hides going for four dollars each in Leverette, three dollars if a buyer picked them up on the range.

The more hides skinned, the bigger the profit. That was elementary. Let the professional hunters keep their pride and their hands clean while they sat around in the afternoon filling up on scootawaboo. Let them pay heavy for extra help just because skinning was beneath them. That was their business.

In Leverette, when the professional hunters laughed at them, it didn't bother Leo Cleary. Maybe they'd get hides, maybe they wouldn't. Either way it didn't matter much. When he thought about it, Leo Cleary believed the boy just wanted to prove a point—that a two-man outfit could make money—attributing it to his Scotch stubbornness. The idea had been Will's dad's—when he was sober. The old man had almost proved it himself.

But whenever anyone laughed, the boy would feel that the laughter was not meant for him but for his father.

Leo Cleary went to work with a frown on his grizzled face, wetting his dry lips disgustedly. He squatted up close to the nearest buffalo and with his skinning knife slit the belly from neck to tail.

He slashed the skin down the inside of each leg, then carved a strip from around the massive neck, his long knife biting at the tough hide close to the head. Then he rose, rubbing the back of his knife hand across his forehead.

"Yo! Will . . ." he called out.

The boy came over then, leading his horse and holding a coiled riata in his free hand. One end was secured to the saddle horn. He bunched the buffalo's heavy neck skin, wrapping the free end of line around it, knotting it.

He led the horse out the whole length of the rope, then mounted, his heels squeezing flanks as soon as he was in the saddle.

"Yiiiiiii!" He screamed in the horse's ear and swatted the rump with his hat. The mount bolted.

The hide held, stretching, then jerked from the carcass, coming with a quick sucking, sliding gasp.

They kept at it through most of the afternoon, sweating over the carcasses, both of them skinning, and butchering some meat for their own use. It was still too early in the year, too warm, to butcher hindquarters for the meat buyers. Later, when the snows came and the meat would keep, they would do this.

They took the fresh hides back to their base camp and staked them out, stretching the skins tightly, flesh side up. The flat ground around the wagon and cook fire was covered with staked-out hides, taken the previous day. In the morning they would gather the hides and bind them in packs and store the packs in the wagon. The boy thought there would be maybe two more days of hunting here before they would have to move the camp.

For the second time that day he stood stretching, rubbing a stiffness in his body, but feeling satisfied. He smiled, and even Leo Cleary wasn't watching him to see it.

At dusk they saw the string of wagons out on the plain, a black line creeping toward them against the sunlight dying on the horizon.

"Hide buyers, most likely," Leo Cleary said. He sounded disappointed, for it could mean they would not return to Leverette for another month.

The boy said, "Maybe a big hunting outfit."

"Not at this time of day," the old man said. "They'd still have their hides drying." He motioned to the creek back of their camp. "Whoever it is, they want water."

Two riders leading the five Conestogas spurred suddenly as they neared the camp and rode in ahead of the six-team wagons. The boy watched them intently. When they were almost to the camp circle, he recognized them and swore under his breath, though he suddenly felt self-conscious.

The Foss brothers, Clyde and Wylie, swung down stiff legged, not waiting for an invitation, and arched the stiffness from their backs. Without a greeting Clyde Foss's eyes roamed leisurely over the staked-out hides, estimating the number as he scratched at his beard stubble. He grinned slowly, looking at his brother.

"They must a used rocks . . . ain't more than forty hides here."

Leo Cleary said, "Hello, Clyde . . . Wylie," and watched the surprise come over them with recognition.

Clyde said, "Damn, Leo, I didn't see you were here. Who's that with you?"

"Matt Gordon's boy," Leo Cleary answered. "We're hunting together this season."

"Just the two of you?" Wylie asked with surprise. He was a few years older than Clyde, calmer, but looked to be his twin. They were both of them lanky, thin through face and body, but heavy boned.

Leo Cleary said, "I thought it was common talk in Leverette about us being out."

"We made up over to Caldwell this year," Clyde said. He looked about the camp again, amused. "Who does the shooting?"

"I do." The boy took a step toward Clyde Foss. His voice was cold, distant. He was thinking of another time four years before when his dad had introduced him to the Foss brothers, the day Matt Gordon contracted with them to pick up his hides.

"And I do skinning," the boy added. It was like

What are you going to do about it! the way he said it.

Clyde laughed again. Wylie just grinned.

"So you're Matt Gordon's boy," Wylie Foss said.

"We met once before."

"We did?"

"In Leverette, four years ago." The boy made himself say it naturally. "A month before you met my dad in the field and paid him for his hides with whiskey instead of cash . . . the day before he was trampled into the ground. . . ."

☆ ☆ ☆

THE FOSS BROTHERS met his stare, and suddenly the amusement was gone from their eyes. Clyde no longer laughed, and Wylie's mouth tightened. Clyde stared at the boy and said, "If you meant anything by that, you better watch your mouth."

Wylie said, "We can't stop buffalo from stampedin'." Clyde grinned now.

"Maybe he's drunk . . . maybe he favors his pa."

"Take it any way you want," the boy said. He stood firmly with his fists clenched. "You knew better than to give him whiskey. You took advantage of him."

Wylie looked up at the rumbling sound of the wagon string coming in, the ponderous creaking of wooden frames, iron-rimmed tires grating, and the never-changing off-key leathery rattle of the traces, then the sound of reins flicking horse hide and the indistinguishable growls of the teamsters.

Wylie moved toward the wagons in the dimness and shouted to the first one, "Ed . . . water down!" pointing toward the creek.

"You bedding here?" Leo Cleary asked after him.

"Just water."

"Moving all night?"

"We're meeting a party on the Salt Fork . . . they ain't going to stay there forever." Wylie Foss walked after the wagons leading away their horses.

Clyde paid little attention to the wagons, only glancing in that direction as they swung toward the stream. Stoop shouldered, his hand curling the brim of his sweat-stained hat, his eyes roamed lazily over the drying hides. He rolled a cigarette, taking his time, failing to offer tobacco to the boy.

"I guess we got room for your hides," he said finally.

"I'm not selling."

"We'll load soon as we water . . . even take the fresh ones."

"I said I'm not selling."

"Maybe I'm not asking."

"There's nothing making me sell if I don't want to!"

The slow smile formed on Clyde's mouth. "You're a mean little fella, aren't you?"

Clyde Foss dropped the cigarette stub and turned

a boot on it. "There's a bottle in my saddle pouch." He nodded to Leo Cleary, who was standing off from them. "Help yourself, Leo."

The old man hesitated.

"I said help yourself."

Leo Cleary moved off toward the stream.

"Now, Mr. Gordon . . . how many hides you say were still dryin'?"

"None for you."

"Forty . . . forty-five?"

"You heard what I said." He was standing close to Clyde Foss, watching his face. He saw the jaw muscles tighten and sensed Clyde's shift of weight. He tried to turn, bringing up his shoulder, but it came with pain-stabbing suddenness. Clyde's fist smashed against his cheek, and he stumbled off balance.

"Forty?"

Clyde's left hand followed around with weight behind it, scraping his temple, staggering him.

"Forty-five?"

He waded after the boy then, clubbing at his face and body, knocking his guard aside to land his fists, until the boy was backed against his wagon. Then Clyde stopped as the boy fell into the wheel spokes, gasping, and slumped to the ground.

Clyde stood over the boy and nudged him with his boot. "Did I hear forty or forty-five?" he said dryly. And when the boy made no answer—"Well, it don't matter."

He heard the wagons coming up from the creek. Wylie was leading the horses. "Boy went to sleep on us, Wylie." He grinned. "He said don't disturb him, just take the skins and leave the payment with Leo." He laughed then. And later, when the wagons pulled out, he was laughing again.

Once he heard voices, a man swearing, a never-ending soft thudding against the ground, noises above him in the wagon. But these passed, and there was nothing.

He woke again, briefly, a piercing ringing in his ears, and his face throbbed violently though the pain seemed to be out from him and not within, as if his face were bloated and would soon burst. He tried to open his mouth, but a weight held his jaws tight. Then wagons moving . . . the sound of traces . . . laughter.

It was still dark when he opened his eyes. The noises had stopped. Something cool was on his face. He felt it with his hand—a damp cloth. He sat up, taking it from his face, working his jaw slowly.

The man was a blur at first . . . something reflecting in his hand. Then it was Leo Cleary, and the something in his hand was a half-empty whiskey bottle.

"There wasn't anything I could do, Will."

"How long they been gone?"

"Near an hour. They took all of them, even the ones staked out." He said, "Will, there wasn't anything I could do. . . ."

"I know," the boy said.

"They paid for the hides with whiskey." The boy looked at him, surprised. He had not expected them to pay anything. But now he saw how this would appeal to Clyde's sense of humor, using the same way the hide buyer had paid his dad four years before.

"That part of it, Leo?" The boy nodded to the whiskey bottle in the old man's hand.

"No, they put three five-gallon barrels in the wagon. Remember . . . Clyde give me this."

The boy was silent. Finally he said, "Don't touch those barrels, Leo."

He sat up the remainder of the night, listening to his thoughts. He had been afraid when Clyde Foss was bullying him, and he was still afraid. But now the fear was mixed with anger, because his body ached and he could feel the loose teeth on one side of his mouth when he tightened his jaw, and taste the blood dry on his lips and most of all because Clyde Foss had taken a month's work, four hundred and eighty hides, and left three barrels of whiskey.

Sometimes the fear was stronger than the anger. The plain was silent and in its darkness there was nothing to hold to. He did not bother Leo Cleary. He talked to himself and listened to the throb in his temples and left Leo alone with the little whiskey he still had. He wanted to cry, but he could not because he had given up the privilege by becoming a man, even though he was still a boy. He was acutely aware of this, and when the urge to cry welled in him he would tighten his nerves and call himself names until the urge passed.

Sometimes the anger was stronger than the fear, and he would think of killing Clyde Foss. Toward morning both the fear and the anger lessened, and many of the things he had thought of during the night he did not now remember. He was sure of only one thing: He was going to get his hides back. A way to do it would come to him. He still had his Sharps.

He shook Leo Cleary awake and told him to hitch the wagon.

"Where we going?" The old man was still dazed, from sleep and whiskey.

"Hunting, Leo. Down on the Salt Fork."

☆ ☆ ☆

HUNTING WAS GOOD in the Nations. The herds would come down from Canada and the Dakotas and winter along the Cimarron and the Salt and even down to the Canadian. Here the herds were big, two and three hundred grazing together, and sometimes you could look over the flat plains and see thousands. A big outfit with a good hunter could average over eighty hides a day. But, because there were so many hunters, the herds kept on the move.

In the evening they saw the first of the buffalo camps. Distant lights in the dimness, then lanterns and cook fires as they drew closer in a dusk turning to night, and the sounds of men drifted out to them on the silent plain.

The hunters and skinners were crouched around a poker game on a blanket, a lantern above them on a crate. They paid little heed to the old man and the boy, letting them prepare their supper on the low-burning cook fire and after, when the boy stood over them and asked questions, they answered him shortly. The game was for high stakes, and there was a pot building. No, they hadn't seen the Foss brothers, and if they had, they wouldn't trade with them anyway. They were taking their skins to Caldwell for top dollar.

They moved on, keeping well off from the flickering line of lights. Will Gordon would go in alone as they neared the camps, and, if there were five wagons in the camp, he'd approach cautiously until he could make out the men at the fire.

From camp to camp it was the same story. Most of the hunters had not seen the Fosses; a few had, earlier in the day, but they could be anywhere now.

Until finally, very late, they talked to a man who had sold to the Foss brothers that morning.

"They even took some fresh hides," he told them.

"Still heading west?" The boy kept his voice even, though he felt the excitement inside of him.

"Part of them," the hunter said. "Wylie went back to Caldwell with three wagons, but Clyde shoved on to meet another party up the Salt. See, Wylie'll come back with empty wagons, and by that time the hunters'll have caught up with Clyde. You ought to find him up a ways. We'll all be up there soon . . . that's where the big herds are heading."

They moved on all night, spelling each other on the wagon box. Leo grumbled and said they were crazy. The boy said little because he was thinking of the big herds. And he was thinking of Clyde Foss with all those hides he had to dry . . . and the plan was forming in his mind.

Leo Cleary watched from the pines, seeing nothing, thinking of the boy who was out somewhere in the darkness, though most of the time he thought of whiskey, barrels of it that they had been hauling for two days and now into the second night.

The boy was a fool. The camp they had seen at sundown was probably just another hunter. They all staked hides at one time or another. Seeing him sneaking up in the dark they could take him for a Kiowa and cut him in two with a buffalo gun. And even if it did turn out to be Clyde Foss, then what?

Later, the boy walked in out of the darkness and pushed the pine branches aside and was standing next to the old man.

"It's Clyde, Leo."

The old man said nothing.

"He's got two men with him."

"So . . . what are you going to do now?" the old man said.

"Hunt," the boy said. He went to his saddlebag and drew a cap-and-ball revolver and loaded it before bedding for the night.

In the morning he took his rifles and led his horse along the base of the ridge, through the pines that were dense here, but scattered higher up the slope. He would look out over the flat plain to the south and see the small squares of canvas, very white in the brilliant sunlight. Ahead, to the west, the ridge dropped off into a narrow valley with timbered hills on the other side.

The boy's eyes searched the plain, roaming to the white squares, Clyde's wagons, but he went on without hesitating until he reached the sloping finish of the ridge. Then he moved up the valley until the plain widened again, and then he stopped to wait. He was prepared to wait for days if necessary, until the right time.

From high up on the slope above, Leo Cleary watched him. Through the morning the old man's eyes would drift from the boy and then off to the left, far out on the plain to the two wagons and the ribbon of river behind them. He tried to relate the boy and the wagons in some way, but he could not.

After a while he saw buffalo. A few straggling off toward the wagons, but even more on the other side of the valley where the plain widened again and the grass was higher, green-brown in the sun.

Toward noon the buffalo increased, and he remembered the hunters saying how the herds were moving west. By that time there were hundreds, perhaps a thousand, scattered over the grass, out a mile or so from the boy who seemed to be concentrating on them.

Maybe he really is going hunting, Leo Cleary thought. Maybe he's starting all over again. But I wish I had me a drink. The boy's downwind now, he thought, lifting his head to feel the breeze on his face. He could edge up and take a hundred of them if he did it right. What's he waiting for! Hell, if he wants to start all over, it's all right with me. I'll stay out with him. At that moment he was thinking of the three barrels of whiskey.

"Go out and get 'em, Will," he urged the boy aloud, though he would not be heard. "The wind won't keep forever!"

Surprised, then, he saw the boy move out from

the brush clumps leading his horse, mount, and lope off in a direction out and away from the herd.

"You can't hunt buffalo from a saddle . . . they'll run as soon as they smell horse! What the hell's the matter with him!"

* * *

HE WATCHED the boy, growing smaller with distance, move out past the herd. Then suddenly the horse wheeled, and it was going at a dead run toward the herd. A yell drifted up to the ridge and then a heavy rifle shot followed by two reports that were weaker. Horse and rider cut into the herd, and the buffalo broke in confusion.

They ran crazily, bellowing, bunching in panic to escape the horse and man smell and the screaming that suddenly hit them with the wind. A herd of buffalo will run for hours if the panic stabs them sharp enough, and they will stay together, bunching their thunder, tons of bulk, massive bellowing heads, horns, and thrashing hooves. Nothing will stop them. Some go down, and the herd passes over, beating them into the ground.

They ran directly away from the smell and the noises that were now far behind, downwind they came and in less than a minute were thundering through the short valley. Dust rose after them, billowing up to the old man, who covered his mouth, coughing, watching the rumbling dark mass erupt from the valley out onto the plain. They moved in an unwavering line toward the Salt Fork, rolling over everything, before swerving at the river—even the two canvas squares that had been brilliant white in the morning sun. And soon they were only a deep hum in the distance.

Will Gordon was out on the flats, approaching the place where the wagons had stood, riding slowly now in the settling dust.

But the dust was still in the air, heavy enough to make Leo Cleary sneeze as he brought the wagon out from the pines toward the river.

He saw the hide buyers' wagons smashed to scrap wood and shredded canvas dragged among the strewn buffalo hides. Many of the bales were still intact, spilling from the wagon wrecks; some were buried under the debris.

Three men stood waist deep in the shallows of the river, and beyond them, upstream, were the horses they had saved. Some had not been cut from the pickets in time, and they lay shapeless in blood at one end of the camp.

Will Gordon stood on the bank with the revolving pistol cocked, pointed at Clyde Foss. He glanced aside as the old man brought up the team.

"He wants to sell back, Leo. How much, you think?"

The old man only looked at him, because he could not speak.

"I think two barrels of whiskey," Will Gordon said. He stepped suddenly into the water and brought the long pistol barrel sweeping against Clyde's head, cutting the temple.

"Two barrels?"

Clyde Foss staggered and came to his feet slowly.

"Come here, Clyde." The boy leveled the pistol at him and waited as Clyde Foss came hesitantly out of the water, hunching his shoulders. The boy swung the pistol back, and, as Clyde ducked, he brought his left fist up, smashing hard against the man's jaw.

"Or three barrels?"

The hide buyer floundered in the shallow water, then crawled to the bank, and lay on his stomach, gasping for breath.

"We'll give him three, Leo. Since he's been nice about it."

Later, after Clyde and his two men had loaded their wagon with four hundred and eighty hides, the old man and the boy rode off through the valley to the great plain.

Once the old man said, "Where we going now, Will?"

And when the boy said, "We're still going hunting, Leo," the old man shrugged wearily and just nodded his head.

6

The Boy Who Smiled

WHEN MICKEY SEGUNDO was fourteen, he tracked a man almost two hundred miles—from the Jicarilla Subagency down into the malpais.

He caught up with him at a water hole in late afternoon and stayed behind a rock outcropping watching the man drink. Mickey Segundo had not tasted water in three days, but he sat patiently behind the cover while the man quenched his thirst, watching him relax and make himself comfortable as the hot lava country cooled with the approach of evening.

Finally Mickey Segundo stirred. He broke open

the .50-caliber Gallagher and inserted the paper cartridge and the cap. Then he eased the carbine between a niche in the rocks, sighting on the back of the man's head. He called in a low voice, "Tony Choddi . . ." and as the face with the wide-open eyes came around, he fired casually.

He lay on his stomach and slowly drank the water he needed, filling his canteen and the one that had belonged to Tony Choddi. Then he took his hunting knife and sawed both of the man's ears off, close to the head. These he put into his saddle pouch, leaving the rest for the buzzards.

A week later Mickey Segundo carried the pouch into the agency office and dropped the ears on my desk. He said very simply, "Tony Choddi is sorry he has caused trouble."

I remember telling him, "You're not thinking of going after McKay now, are you?"

"This man, Tony Choddi, stole stuff, a horse and clothes and a gun," he said with his pleasant smile. "So I thought I would do a good thing and fix it so Tony Choddi didn't steal no more."

With the smile there was a look of surprise, as if to say, "Why would I want to get Mr. McKay?"

A few days later I saw McKay and told him about it and mentioned that he might keep his eyes open. But he said that he didn't give a damn about any breed Jicarilla kid. If the kid felt like avenging his old man, he could try, but he'd probably cash in before his time. And as for getting Tony Choddi, he didn't give a damn about that either. He'd got the horse back and that's all he cared about.

After he had said his piece, I was sorry I had warned him. And I felt a little foolish telling one of the biggest men in the Territory to look out for a half-breed Apache kid. I told myself, Maybe you're just rubbing up to him because he's important and could use his influence to help out the agency . . . and maybe he knows it.

Actually I had more respect for Mickey Segundo, as a human being, than I did for T. O. McKay. Maybe I felt I owed the warning to McKay because he was a white man. Like saying, "Mickey Segundo's a good boy, but, hell, he's half Indian." Just one of those things you catch yourself doing. Like habit. You do something wrong the first time and you know it, but if you keep it up, it becomes a habit and it's no longer wrong because it's something you've always been doing.

McKay and a lot of people said Apaches were no damn good. The only good one was a dead one. They never stopped to reason it out. They'd been saying it so long, they knew it was true. Certainly any such statement was unreasonable, but damned if I wouldn't sometimes nod my head in agreement, because at those times I'd be with white men and that's the way white men talked.

I might have thought I was foolish, but actually it

was McKay who was the fool. He underestimated Mickey Segundo.

That was five years ago. It had begun with a hanging.

★ ★ ★

EARLY IN THE morning, Tudishishn, sergeant of Apache police at the Jicarilla Agency, rode in to tell me that Tony Choddi had jumped the boundaries again and might be in my locale. Tudishishn stayed for half a dozen cups of coffee, though his information didn't last that long. When he'd had enough, he left as leisurely as he had arrived. Hunting renegades, reservation jumpers, was Tudishishn's job; still, it wasn't something to get excited about. Tomorrows were for work; todays were for thinking about it.

Up at the agency they were used to Tony Choddi skipping off. Usually they'd find him later in some shaded barranca, full of tulapai.

It was quiet until late afternoon, but not unusually so. It wasn't often that anything out of the ordinary happened at the subagency. There were twenty-six families, one hundred eight Jicarillas all told, under my charge. We were located almost twenty miles below the reservation proper, and most of the people had been there long before the reservation had been marked off. They had been fairly peaceful then, and remained so now. It was one of the few instances where the Bureau allowed the sleeping dog to lie; and because of that we had less trouble than they did up at the reservation.

There was a sign on the door of the adobe office which described it formally. It read: D. J. MERRITT—AGENT, JICARILLA APACHE SUBAGENCY—PUERCO, NEW MEXICO TERRITORY. It was a startling announcement to post on the door of a squat adobe sitting all alone in the shadow of the Nacimentos. My Apaches preferred higher ground and the closest jacales were two miles up into the foothills. The office had to remain on the mail run, even though the mail consisted chiefly of impossible-to-apply Bureau memoranda.

Just before supper Tudishishn returned. He came in at a run this time and swung off before his pony had come to a full stop. He was excited and spoke in a confusion of Apache, Spanish, and a word here and there of English.

Returning to the reservation, he had decided to stop off and see his friends of the Puerco Agency. There had been friends he had not seen for some time, and the morning had lengthened into afternoon with tulapai, good talking, and even coffee. People had come from the more remote jacales, deeper in the hills, when they learned Tudishishn was there, to hear news of friends at the reservation. Soon there were many people and what looked like the beginning of a good time. Then Señor McKay had come.

McKay had men with him, many men, and they were looking for Mickey Solner—the squaw man, as the Americans called him.

Most of the details I learned later on, but briefly this is what had happened: McKay and some of his men were out on a hunting trip. When they got up that morning, McKay's horse was gone, along with a shotgun and some personal articles. They got on the tracks, which were fresh and easy to follow, and by that afternoon they were at Mickey Solner's jacale. His woman and boy were there, and the horse was tethered in front of the mud hut. Mickey Segundo, the boy, was honored to lead such important people to his father, who was visiting with Tudishishn.

McKay brought the horse along, and when they found Mickey Solner, they took hold of him without asking questions and looped a rope around his neck. Then they boosted him up onto the horse they claimed he had stolen. McKay said it would be fitting that way. Tudishishn had left fast when he saw what was about to happen. He knew they wouldn't waste time arguing with an Apache, so he had come to me.

When I got there, Mickey Solner was still sitting McKay's chestnut mare with the rope reaching from his neck to the cottonwood bough overhead. His head drooped as if all the fight was out of him, and when I came up in front of the chestnut, he looked at me with tired eyes, watery and red from tulapai.

I had known Solner for years, but had never become close to him. He wasn't a man with whom you became fast friends. Just his living in an Apache rancheria testified to his being of a different breed. He was friendly enough, but few of the whites liked him—they said he drank all the time and never worked. Maybe most were just envious. Solner was a white man gone Indian, whole hog. That was the cause of the resentment.

His son, Mickey the Second, stood near his dad's stirrup looking at him with a bewildered, pathetic look on his slim face. He held on to the stirrup as if he'd never let it go. And it was the first time, the only time, I ever saw Mickey Segundo without a faint smile on his face.

"Mr. McKay," I said to the cattleman, who was standing relaxed with his hands in his pockets, "I'm afraid I'll have to ask you to take that man down. He's under bureau jurisdiction and will have to be tried by a court."

McKay said nothing, but Bowie Allison, who was his herd boss, laughed and then said, "You ought to be afraid."

Dolph Bettzinger was there, along with his brothers Kirk and Sim. They were hired for their guns and usually kept pretty close to McKay. They did not laugh when Allison did.

And all around the clearing by the cottonwood were eight or ten others. Most of them I recognized as McKay riders. They stood solemnly, some with rifles and shotguns. There wasn't any doubt in their minds what stealing a horse meant.

"Tudishishn says that Mickey didn't steal your horse. These people told him that he was at home all night and most of the morning until Tudishishn dropped in, and then he came down here." A line of Apaches stood a few yards off and as I pointed to them, some nodded their heads.

"Mister," McKay said, "I found the horse at this man's hut. Now, you argue that down, and I'll kiss the behind of every Apache you got living around here."

"Well, your horse could have been left there by someone else."

"Either way, he had a hand in it," he said curtly.

"What does he say?" I looked up at Mickey Solner and asked him quickly, "How did you get the horse, Mickey?"

"I just traded with a fella." His voice shook, and he held on to the saddle horn as if afraid he'd fall off. "This fella come along and traded with me, that's all."

"Who was it?"

Mickey Solner didn't answer. I asked him again, but still he refused to speak. McKay was about to say something, but Tudishishn came over quickly from the group of Apaches.

"They say it was Tony Choddi. He was seen to come into camp in early morning."

I asked Mickey if it was Tony Choddi, and finally he admitted that it was. I felt better then. McKay couldn't hang a man for trading a horse.

"Are you satisfied, Mr. McKay? He didn't know it was yours. Just a matter of trading a horse."

McKay looked at me, narrowing his eyes. He looked as if he were trying to figure out what kind of a man I was. Finally he said, "You think I'm going to believe them?"

It dawned on me suddenly that McKay had been using what patience he had for the past few minutes. Now he was ready to continue what they had come for. He had made up his mind long before.

"Wait a minute, Mr. McKay, you're talking about the life of an innocent man. You can't just toy with it like it was a head of cattle."

He looked at me and his puffy face seemed to harden. He was a heavy man, beginning to sag about the stomach. "You think you're going to tell me what I can do and what I can't? I don't need a government representative to tell me why my horse was stolen!"

"I'm not telling you anything. You know Mickey didn't steal the horse. You can see for yourself you're making a mistake."

McKay shrugged and looked at his herd boss. "Well, if it is, it isn't a very big one—leastwise we'll be sure he won't be trading in stolen horses again." He nodded to Bowie Allison.

Bowie grinned, and brought his quirt up and then down across the rump of the chestnut.

"Yiiiiiiiii . . ."

The chestnut broke fast. Allison stood yelling after it, then jumped aside quickly as Mickey Solner swung back toward him on the end of the rope.

* * *

IT WAS TWO weeks later, to the day, that Mickey Segundo came in with Tony Choddi's ears. You can see why I asked him if he had a notion of going after McKay. And it was a strange thing. I was talking to a different boy than the one I had last seen under the cottonwood.

When the horse shot out from under his dad, he ran to him like something wild, screaming, and wrapped his arms around the kicking legs trying to hold the weight off the rope.

Bowie Allison cuffed him away, and they held him back with pistols while he watched his dad die. From then on he didn't say a word, and when it was over, walked away with his head down. Then, when he came in with Tony Choddi's ears, he was himself again. All smiles.

I might mention that I wrote to the Bureau of Indian Affairs about the incident, since Mickey Solner, legally, was one of my charges; but nothing came of it. In fact, I didn't even get a reply.

Over the next few years Mickey Segundo changed a lot. He became Apache. That is, his appearance changed and almost everything else about him—except the smile. The smile was always there, as if he knew a monumental secret which was going to make everyone happy.

He let his hair grow to his shoulders and usually he wore only a frayed cotton shirt and breechclout; his moccasins were Apache—curled toes and leggings which reached to his thighs. He went under his Apache name, which was Peza-a, but I called him Mickey when I saw him, and he was never reluctant to talk to me in English. His English was good, discounting grammar.

Most of the time he lived in the same jacale his dad had built, providing for his mother and fitting closer into the life of the rancheria than he did before. But when he was about eighteen, he went up to the agency and joined Tudishishn's police. His mother went with him to live at the reservation, but within a year the two of them were back. Tracking friends who happened to wander off the reservation didn't set right with him. It didn't go with his smile.

Tudishishn told me he was sorry to lose him because he was an expert tracker and a dead shot. I know the sergeant had a dozen good sign followers, but very few who were above average with a gun.

He must have been nineteen when he came back to Puerco. In all those years he never once mentioned McKay's name. And I can tell you I never brought it up either.

I saw McKay even less after the hanging incident. If he ignored me before, he avoided me now. As I said, I felt like a fool after warning him about Mickey Segundo, and I'm certain McKay felt only contempt for me for doing it, after sticking up for the boy's dad.

McKay would come through every once in a while, usually going on a hunt up into the Nacimentos. He was a great hunter and would go out for a few days every month or so. Usually with his herd boss, Bowie Allison. He hunted everything that walked, squirmed, or flew and I'm told his ranch trophy room was really something to see.

You couldn't take it away from the man; everything he did, he did well. He was in his fifties, but he could shoot straighter and stay in the saddle longer than any of his riders. And he knew how to make money. But it was his arrogance that irked me. Even though he was polite, he made you feel far beneath him. He talked to you as if you were one of the hired help.

One afternoon, fairly late, Tudishishn rode in and said that he was supposed to meet McKay at the adobe office early the next morning. McKay wanted to try the shooting down southwest toward the malpais, on the other side of it, actually, and Tudishishn was going to guide for him.

The Indian policeman drank coffee until almost sundown and then rode off into the shadows of the Nacimentos. He was staying at one of the rancherias, visiting with his friends until the morning.

McKay appeared first. It was a cool morning, bright and crisp. I looked out of the window and saw the five riders coming up the road from the south, and when they were close enough I made out McKay and Bowie Allison and the three Bettzinger brothers. When they reached the office, McKay and Bowie dismounted, but the Bettzingers reined around and started back down the road.

McKay nodded and was civil enough, though he didn't direct more than a few words to me. Bowie was ready when I asked them if they wanted coffee, but McKay shook his head and said they were leaving shortly. Just about then the rider appeared coming down out of the hills.

McKay was squinting, studying the figure on the pony.

I didn't really look at him until I noticed McKay's close attention. And when I looked at the rider again, he was almost on us. I didn't have to squint then to see that it was Mickey Segundo.

McKay said, "Who's that?" with a ring of suspicion to his voice.

I felt a sudden heat on my face, like the feeling

you get when you're talking about someone, then suddenly find the person standing next to you.

Without thinking about it I told McKay, "That's Peza-a, one of my people." What made me call him by his Apache name I don't know. Perhaps because he looked so Indian. But I had never called him Peza-a before.

He approached us somewhat shyly, wearing his faded shirt and breechclout but now with a streak of ochre painted across his nose from ear to ear. He didn't look as if he could have a drop of white blood in him.

"What's he doing here?" McKay's voice still held a note of suspicion, and he looked at him as if he were trying to place him.

Bowie Allison studied him the same way, saying nothing.

"Where's Tudishishn? These gentlemen are waiting for him."

"Tudishishn is ill with a demon in his stomach," Peza-a answered. "He has asked me to substitute myself for him." He spoke in Spanish, hesitantly, the way an Apache does.

McKay studied him for some time. Finally, he said, "Well . . . can he track?"

"He was with Tudishishn for a year. Tudishishn speaks highly of him." Again I don't know what made me say it. A hundred things were going through my head. What I said was true, but I saw it getting me into something. Mickey never looked directly at me. He kept watching McKay, with the faint smile on his mouth.

McKay seemed to hesitate, but then he said, "Well, come on. I don't need a reference . . . long as he can track."

They mounted and rode out.

McKay wanted prongbuck. Tudishishn had described where they would find the elusive herds and promised to show him all he could shoot. But they were many days away. McKay had said if he didn't have time, he'd make time. He wanted good shooting.

Off and on during the first day he questioned Mickey Segundo closely to see what he knew about the herds.

"I have seen them many times. Their hide the color of sand, and black horns that reach into the air like bayonets of the soldiers. But they are far."

McKay wasn't concerned with distance. After a while he was satisfied that this Indian guide knew as much about tracking antelope as Tudishishn, and that's what counted. Still, there was something about the young Apache. . . .

★ ★ ★

"TOMORROW, WE begin the crossing of the malpais," Mickey Segundo said. It was evening of the third day, as they made camp at Yucca Springs.

Bowie Allison looked at him quickly. "Tudishishn planned we'd follow the high country down and come out on the plain from the east."

"What's the matter with keeping a straight line," McKay said. "Keeping to the hills is longer, isn't it?"

"Yeah, but that malpais is a blood-dryin' furnace in the middle of August," Bowie grumbled. "You got to be able to pinpoint the wells. And even if you find them, they might be dry."

McKay looked at Peza-a for an answer.

"If Señor McKay wishes to ride for two additional days, that is for him to say. But we can carry our water with ease." He went to his saddle pouch and drew out two collapsed, rubbery bags. "These, from the stomach of the horse, will hold much water. Tomorrow we fill canteens and these, and the water can be made to last five, six days. Even if the wells are dry, we have water."

Bowie Allison grumbled under his breath, looking with distaste at the horse-intestine water sacks.

McKay rubbed his chin thoughtfully. He was thinking of prongbuck. Finally he said, "We'll cut across the lava."

Bowie Allison was right in his description of the malpais. It was a furnace, a crusted expanse of desert that stretched into another world. Saguaro and ocotillo stood nakedly sharp against the whiteness, and off in the distance were ghostly looming buttes, gigantic tombstones for the lava waste. Horses shuffled choking white dust, and the sun glare was a white blistering shock that screamed its brightness. Then the sun would drop suddenly, leaving a nothingness that could be felt. A life that had died a hundred million years ago.

McKay felt it and that night he spoke little.

The second day was a copy of the first, for the lava country remained monotonously the same. McKay grew more irritable as the day wore on, and time and again he would snap at Bowie Allison for his grumbling. The country worked at the nerves of the two white men, while Mickey Segundo watched them.

On the third day they passed two water holes. They could see the shallow crusted bottoms and the fissures that the tight sand had made cracking in the hot air. That night McKay said nothing.

In the morning there was a blue haze on the edge of the glare; they could feel the land beneath them begin to rise. Chaparral and patches of toboso grass became thicker and dotted the flatness, and by early afternoon the towering rock formations loomed near at hand. They had then one water sack two thirds full; but the other, with their canteens, was empty.

Bowie Allison studied the gradual rise of the rock wall, passing his tongue over cracked lips. "There could be water up there. Sometimes the rain catches in hollows and stays there a long time if it's shady."

McKay squinted into the air. The irregular crests were high and dead still against the sky. "Could be."

Mickey Segundo looked up and then nodded.

"How far to the next hole?" McKay asked.

"Maybe one day."

"If it's got water. . . . Then how far?"

"Maybe two day. We come out on the plain then near the Datil Mountains and there is water, streams to be found."

McKay said, "That means we're halfway. We can make last what we got, but there's no use killing ourselves." His eyes lifted to the peaks again, then dropped to the mouth of a barranca which cut into the rock. He nodded to the dark canyon which was partly hidden by a dense growth of mesquite. "We'll leave our stuff there and go on to see what we can find."

They unsaddled the horses and ground-tied them and hung their last water bag in the shade of a mesquite bush.

Then they walked up-canyon until they found a place which would be the easiest to climb.

They went up and they came down, but when they were again on the canyon floor, their canteens still rattled lightly with their steps. Mickey Segundo carried McKay's rifle in one hand and the limp, empty water bag in the other.

He walked a step behind the two men and watched their faces as they turned to look back overhead. There was no water.

The rocks held nothing, not even a dampness. They were naked now and loomed brutally indifferent, and bone dry with no promise of moisture.

The canyon sloped gradually into the opening. And now, ahead, they could see the horses and the small fat bulge of the water bag hanging from the mesquite bough.

Mickey Segundo's eyes were fixed on the water sack. He looked steadily at it.

Then a horse screamed. They saw the horses suddenly pawing the ground and pulling at the hackamores that held them fast. The three horses and the pack mule joined together now, neighing shrilly as they strained dancing at the ropes.

And then a shape the color of sand darted through the mesquite thicket, so quickly that it seemed a shadow.

Mickey Segundo threw the rifle to his shoulder. He hesitated. Then he fired.

The shape kept going, past the mesquite background and out into the open.

He fired again and the coyote went up into the air and came down to lie motionless.

It only jerked in death. McKay looked at him angrily. "Why the hell didn't you let me have it! You could have hit one of the horses!"

"There was not time."

"That's two hundred yards! You could have hit a horse, that's what I'm talking about!"

"But I shot it," Mickey Segundo said.

When they reached the mesquite clump, they did not go over to inspect the dead coyote. Something else took their attention. It stopped the white men in their tracks.

They stared unbelieving at the wetness seeping into the sand, and above the spot, the water bag hanging like a punctured bladder. The water had quickly run out.

Mickey Segundo told the story at the inquiry. They had attempted to find water, but it was no use; so they were compelled to try to return.

They had almost reached Yucca Springs when the two men died. Mickey Segundo told it simply. He was sorry he had shot the water bag, but what could he say? God directs the actions of men in mysterious ways.

The county authorities were disconcerted, but they had to be satisfied with the apparent facts.

McKay and Allison were found ten miles from Yucca Springs and brought in. There were no marks of violence on either of them, and they found three hundred dollars in McKay's wallet. It was officially recorded that they died from thirst and exposure.

A terrible way to die just because some damn Apache couldn't shoot straight. Peza-a survived because he was lucky, along with the fact that he was Apache, which made him tougher. Just one of those things.

Mickey continued living with his mother at the subagency. His old Gallagher carbine kept them in meat, and they seemed happy enough just existing.

Tudishishn visited them occasionally, and when he did they would have a tulapai party. Everything was normal.

Mickey's smile was still there but maybe a little different.

But I've often wondered what Mickey Segundo would have done if that coyote had not run across the mesquite thicket. . . .

7

Only Good Ones

PICTURE THE GROUND rising on the east side of the pasture with scrub trees thick on the slope and pines higher up. This is where everybody was. Not all in one place but scattered in small groups: about a dozen men in the scrub, the front-line men, the shooters who couldn't just stand around. They'd fire at the shack when they felt like it or, when Mr. Tanner passed the word, they would all fire at once. Other people were up in the pines and on the road which ran along the crest of the hill, some three hundred yards from the shack across the pasture.

Those watching made bets whether the man in the shack would give himself up or get shot first.

It was Saturday and that's why everybody had the time. They would arrive in town that morning, hear about what had happened, and, shortly after, head out to the cattle-company pasture. Almost all of the men went out alone, leaving their families in town: though there were a few women who came. The other women waited. And the people who had business in town and couldn't leave waited. Now and then somebody came back to have a drink or their dinner and would tell what was going on. No, they hadn't got him yet. Still inside the line shack and not showing his face.

But they'd get him. A few more would go out when they heard this. Also a wagon from De Spain's went out with whiskey. That's how the saloon was set up in the pines overlooking the pasture and why nobody went back to town after that.

Barely a mile from town those going out would hear the gunfire, like a skirmish way over on the other side of a woods, thin specks of sound, and this would hurry them. They were careful, though, topping the slope, looking across the pasture, getting their bearings, then peering to see who was present. They would see a friend and ask about this Mr. Tanner and the friend would point him out.

The man there in the dark suit: thin and bony,

not big but looking like he was made of gristle and hard to kill, with a mustache and a thin nose and a dark dusty hat worn square over his eyes. That was him. Nobody had ever seen him before that morning. They would look at Mr. Tanner, then across the pasture again to the line shack three hundred yards away. It was a little bake-oven of a hut, wood framed and made of sod and built against a rise where there were pines so the hut would be in shade part of the day. There were no windows in the hut, no gear lying around to show anybody lived there. The hut stood in the sun now with its door closed, the door chipped and splintered by all the bullets that had poured into it and through it.

Off to the right where the pine shapes against the sky rounded and became willows, there in the trees by the creek bed, was the man's wagon and team. In the wagon were the supplies he had bought that morning in town before Mr. Tanner spotted him.

Out in front of the hut, about ten or fifteen feet, was something on the ground. From the slope three hundred yards away nobody could tell what it was until a man came who had field glasses. He looked up and said, frowning, it was a doll: one made of cloth scraps, a stuffed doll with buttons for eyes.

The woman must have dropped it, somebody said.

The woman? the man with the field glasses said.

A Lipan Apache woman who was his wife or his woman or just with him. Mr. Tanner hadn't been clear about that. All they knew was she was in the hut with him and if the man wanted her to stay and get shot, that was his business.

Bob Valdez, twenty years old and town constable for three weeks, carrying a shotgun and glad he had something to hold on to, was present at the Maricopa pasture. He arrived about noon. He told Mr. Tanner who he was, speaking quietly and waiting for Mr. Tanner to answer. Mr. Tanner nodded but did not shake hands and turned away to say something to an R.L. Davis, who rode for Maricopa when he was working. Bob Valdez stood there and didn't know what to do.

He watched the two men. Two of a kind, uh? Both cut from the same stringy hide and looking like father and son: Tanner talking, never smiling, hardly moving his mouth; R.L. Davis standing hip-cocked, posing with his revolver and rifle and a cartridge belt over his shoulder and the funneled, pointed brim of his sweaty hat nodding up and down as he listened to Mr. Tanner, smiling at what Mr. Tanner said, laughing out loud while still Mr. Tanner did not even show the twitch of a lip. Bob Valdez did not like R.L. Davis or any of the R.L. Davises he had met. He was civil, he listened to them, but, God, there were a lot of them to listen to.

A Mr. Beaudry, who leased land to the cattle company, was there. Also Mr. Malsom, manager of Maricopa, and a horsebreaker by the name of

Diego Luz, who was big for a Mexican but never offensive and he drank pretty well.

Mr. Beaudry, nodding and also squinting so he could picture the man inside the line shack, said, "There was something peculiar about him. I mean having a name like Orlando Rincon."

"He worked for me," Mr. Malsom said. He was looking at Mr. Tanner. "I mistrusted him and I believe that was part of it, his name being Orlando Rincon."

"Johnson," Mr. Tanner said.

"I hired him two, three times," Mr. Malsom said. "For heavy work. When I had work you couldn't kick a man to doing."

"His name is Johnson," Mr. Tanner said. "There is no fuzz-head by the name of Orlando Rincon. I'm telling you, this one is a fuzz-head from the Fort Huachuca Tenth fuzz-head cavalry and his name was Johnson when he killed James C. Baxter a year ago and nothing else."

He spoke as you might speak to young children to press something into their minds. This man had no warmth and he was probably not very smart. But there was no reason to doubt him.

Bob Valdez kept near Mr. Tanner because he was the center of what was going on here. They would discuss the situation and decide what to do. As the law-enforcement man he, Bob Valdez, should be in on the discussion and the decision. If someone was to arrest Orlando Rincon or Johnson or whatever his name was, then he should do it; he was town constable. They were out of town maybe, but where did the town end? The town had moved out here now; it was the same thing.

Wait for Rincon to give up. Then arrest him.

If he wasn't dead already.

"Mr. Malsom." Bob Valdez stepped toward the cattle-company manager, who glanced over but looked out across the pasture again, indifferent.

"I wondered if maybe he's already dead," Valdez said.

Mr. Malsom, standing heavier and taller and twenty years older than Bob Valdez, said, "Why don't you find out?"

"I was thinking," Valdez said, "if he was dead we could stand here a long time."

R. L. Davis adjusted his hat, which he did often, grabbing the funneled brim, loosening it on his head and pulling it down close to his eyes again and shifting from one cocked hip to the other. "This constable here's got better things to do," R. L. Davis said. "He's busy."

"No," Bob Valdez said. "I was thinking of the man, Rincon. He's dead or he's alive. He's alive maybe he wants to give himself up. In there he has time to think, uh? Maybe—" He stopped. Not one of them was listening. Not even R. L. Davis.

Mr. Malsom was looking at the whiskey wagon;

it was on the road above them and over a little ways with men standing by it, being served off the tailgate. "I think we could use something," Mr. Malsom said. His gaze went to Diego Luz the horsebreaker, and Diego straightened up; not much, but a little. He was heavy and very dark and his shirt was tight across the thickness of his body. They said that Diego Luz hit green horses on the muzzle with his fist and they minded him. He had the hands for it; they hung at his sides, not touching or fooling with anything. They turned open, gestured, when Mr. Malsom told him to get the whiskey and as he moved off, climbing the slope, one hand held his holstered revolver to his leg.

Mr. Malsom looked up at the sky, squinting and taking his hat off and putting it on again. He took off his coat and held it hooked over his shoulder by one finger, said something, gestured, and he and Mr. Beaudry and Mr. Tanner moved a few yards down the slope to a hollow where there was good shade. It was about two or two-thirty then, hot, fairly still and quiet considering the number of people there. Only some of them in the pines and down in the scrub could be seen from where Bob Valdez stood wondering whether he should follow the three men down to the hollow. Or wait for Diego Luz, who was at the whiskey wagon now, where most of the sounds that carried came from: a voice, a word or two that was suddenly clear, or laughter, and people would look up to see what was going on. Some of them by the whiskey wagon had lost interest in the line shack. Others were still watching, though: those farther along the road sitting in wagons and buggies. This was a day, a date, uh? that people would remember and talk about. Sure, I was there, the man in the buggy would be saying a year from now in a saloon over in Benson or St. David or somewhere. The day they got that army deserter, he had a Big-Fifty Sharps and an old Walker and I'll tell you it was ticklish business.

Down in that worn-out pasture, dusty and spotted with desert growth, prickly pear and brittlebush, there was just the sun. It showed the ground cleanly all the way to just in front of the line shack where now, toward the midafternoon, there was shadow coming out from the trees and from the mound the hut was set against.

Somebody in the scrub must have seen the door open. The shout came from there, and Bob Valdez and everybody on the slope was looking by the time the Lipan Apache woman had reached the edge of the shade. She walked out from the hut toward the willow trees carrying a bucket, not hurrying or even looking toward the slope.

Nobody fired at her; though this was not so strange. Putting the front sight on a sod hut and on a person are two different things. The men in the scrub and in the pines didn't know this woman.

They weren't after her. She had just appeared. There she was; and no one was sure what to do about her.

She was in the trees a while by the creek, then she was in the open again, walking back toward the hut with the bucket and not hurrying at all: a small figure way across the pasture almost without shape or color, with only the long skirt reaching to the ground to tell it was the woman.

So he's alive, Bob Valdez thought. And he wants to stay alive and he's not giving himself up.

He thought about the woman's nerve and whether Orlando Rincon had sent her out or she had decided this herself. You couldn't tell about an Indian woman. Maybe this was expected of her. The woman didn't count; the man did. You could lose the woman and get another one.

Mr. Tanner didn't look at R. L. Davis. His gaze held on the Lipan Apache woman, inched along with her toward the hut; but must have known R. L. Davis was right next to him.

"She's saying she don't give a goddamn about you and your rifle," Mr. Tanner said.

R. L. Davis looked at him funny. Then he said, "Shoot her?" Like he hoped that's what Mr. Tanner meant.

"Well, you could make her jump some," Mr. Tanner said.

Now R. L. Davis was onstage and he knew it and

Bob Valdez could tell he knew it by the way he levered the Winchester, raised it, and fired all in one motion, and as the dust kicked behind the Indian woman, who kept walking and didn't look up, R. L. Davis fired and fired and fired as fast as he could lever and half aim and with everybody watching him, hurrying him, he put four good ones right behind the woman. His last bullet socked into the door just as she reached it and now she did pause and look up at the slope, staring up like she was waiting for him to fire again and giving him a good target if he wanted it.

Mr. Malsom laughed out loud. "She still don't give a goddamn about your rifle."

It stung R. L. Davis, which it was intended to do. "I wasn't aiming at her!"

"But she doesn't know that." Mr. Malsom was grinning, turning then and reaching out a hand as Diego Luz approached them with the whiskey.

"Hell, I wanted to hit her she'd be laying there, you know it."

"Well, now, you go tell her that," Mr. Malsom said, working the cork loose, "and she'll know it." He took a drink from the bottle and passed it to Mr. Beaudry, who drank and handed the bottle to Mr. Tanner. Mr. Tanner did not drink; he passed the bottle to R. L. Davis, who was standing, staring at Mr. Malsom. Finally R. L. Davis jerked the bottle up, took a long swallow, and that part was over.

Mr. Malsom said to Mr. Tanner, "You don't want any?"

"Not today," Mr. Tanner answered. He continued to stare out across the pasture.

Mr. Malsom watched him. "You feel strongly about this army deserter."

"I told you," Mr. Tanner said, "he killed a man was a friend of mine."

"No, I don't believe you did."

"James C. Baxter of Fort Huachuca," Mr. Tanner said. "He come across a *tulapai* still this nigger soldier was working with some Indians. The nigger thought Baxter would tell the army people, so he shot him and ran off with a woman."

"And you saw him this morning."

"I had come in last night and stopped off, going to Tucson," Mr. Tanner said. "This morning I was getting ready to leave when I saw him; him and the woman."

"I was right there," R. L. Davis said. "Right, Mr. Tanner? Him and I were on the porch by the Republic and Rincon goes by in the wagon. Mr. Tanner said, 'You know that man?' I said, 'Only that he's lived up north of town a few months. Him and the woman.' 'Well, I know him,' Mr. Tanner said. 'That man's an army deserter wanted for murder.' I said, 'Well, let's go get him.' He had a start on us and that's how he got to the hut before we could grab on to him. He's been holed up ever since."

Mr. Malsom said, "Then you didn't talk to him."

"Listen," Mr. Tanner said, "I've kept that man's face before my eyes this past year."

Bob Valdez, somewhat behind Mr. Tanner and to the side, moved in a little closer. "You know this is the same man, uh?"

Mr. Tanner looked around. He stared at Valdez. That's all he did—just stared.

"I mean, we have to be sure," Bob Valdez said. "It's a serious thing."

Now Mr. Malsom and Mr. Beaudry were looking up at him. "We," Mr. Beaudry said. "I'll tell you what, Roberto. We need help we'll call you. All right?"

"You hired me," Bob Valdez said, standing alone above them. He was serious but he shrugged and smiled a little to take the edge off the words. "What did you hire me for?"

"Well," Mr. Beaudry said, acting it out, looking past Bob Valdez and along the road both ways, "I was to see some drunk Mexicans I'd point them out."

A person can be in two different places and he will be two different people. Maybe if you think of some more places the person will be more people, but don't take it too far. This is Bob Valdez standing by himself with the shotgun and having only the shotgun to hold on to. This is one Bob Valdez. About twenty years old. Mr. Beaudry and others could try and think of a time when Bob Valdez might have drunk too much or swaggered or had a certain smart look on his face, but they would never recall such a time. This Bob Valdez was all right.

Another Bob Valdez inside the Bob Valdez at the pasture that day worked for the army one time and was a guide when Crook chased Chato and Chihuahua down into the Madres. He was seventeen then, with a Springfield and Apache moccasins that came up to his knees. He would sit at night with the Apache scouts from San Carlos, eating with them and talking some as he learned Chiricahua. He would keep up with them all day and shoot the Springfield one hell of a lot better than any of them could shoot. He came home with a scalp but never showed it to anyone and had thrown it away by the time he went to work for Maricopa. Shortly after that he was named town constable at twenty-five dollars a month, getting the job because he got along with people: the Mexicans in town who drank too much on Saturday night liked him and that was the main thing.

The men with the whiskey bottle had forgotten Valdez. They stayed in the hollow where the shade was cool watching the line shack and waiting for the army deserter to realize it was all up with him. He would realize it and open the door and be cut down as he came outside. It was a matter of time only.

Bob Valdez stayed on the open part of the slope

that was turning to shade, sitting now like an Apache and every once in a while making a cigarette and smoking it slowly as he thought about himself and Mr. Tanner and the others, then thinking about the army deserter.

Diego Luz came and squatted next to him, his arms on his knees and his big hands that he used for breaking horses hanging in front of him.

"Stay near if they want you for something," Valdez said. He was watching Beaudry tilt the bottle up. Diego Luz said nothing.

"One of them bends over," Bob Valdez said then, "you kiss it, uh?"

Diego Luz looked at him, patient about it. Not mad or even stirred up. "Why don't you go home?"

"He says Get me a bottle, you run."

"I get it. I don't run."

"Smile and hold your hat, uh?"

"And don't talk so much."

"Not unless they talk to you first."

"You better go home," Diego said.

Bob Valdez said, "That's why you hit the horses."

"Listen," Diego Luz said, scowling a bit now. "They pay me to break horses. They pay you to talk to drunks on Saturday night and keep them from killing somebody. They don't pay you for what you think or how you feel, so if you take their money, keep your mouth shut. All right?"

Diego Luz got up and walked away, down toward the hollow. The hell with this kid, he was thinking. He'll learn or he won't learn, but the hell with him. He was also thinking that maybe he could get a drink from that bottle. Maybe there'd be a half inch left nobody wanted and Mr. Malsom would tell him to kill it.

But it was already finished. R. L. Davis was playing with the bottle, holding it by the neck and flipping it up and catching it as it came down. Beaudry was saying, "What about after dark?" Looking at Mr. Tanner, who was thinking about something else and didn't notice. R L. Davis stopped flipping the bottle. He said, "Put some men on the rise right above the hut; he comes out, bust him."

"Well, they should get the men over there," Mr. Beaudry said, looking at the sky. "It won't be long till dark."

"Where's he going?" Mr. Malsom said.

The others looked up, stopped in whatever they were doing or thinking by the suddenness of Mr. Malsom's voice.

"Hey, Valdez!" R. L. Davis yelled out. "Where do you think you're going?"

Bob Valdez had circled them and was already below them on the slope, leaving the pines now and entering the scrub brush. He didn't stop or look back.

"Valdez!"

Mr. Tanner raised one hand to silence R. L. Davis, all the time watching Bob Valdez getting smaller, going straight through the scrub, not just walking or passing the time but going right out to the pasture.

"Look at him," Mr. Malsom said. There was some admiration in the voice.

"He's dumber than he looks," R. L. Davis said. Then jumped a little as Mr. Tanner touched his arm.

"Come on," Mr. Tanner said. "With a rifle." And started down the slope, hurrying and not seeming to care if he might stumble on the loose gravel.

Bob Valdez was now halfway across the pasture, the shotgun pointed down at his side, his eyes not leaving the door of the line shack. The door was probably already open enough for a rifle barrel to poke through. He guessed the army deserter was covering him, letting him get as close as he wanted; the closer he came, the easier to hit him.

Now he could see all the bullet marks in the door and the clean inner wood where the door was splintered. Two people in that little bake-oven of a place. He saw the door move.

He saw the rag doll on the ground. It was a strange thing, the woman having a doll. Valdez hardly glanced at it but was aware of the button eyes looking up and the discomforted twist of the red wool mouth. Then, just past the doll, when he was wondering if he would go right up to the door and knock on it and wouldn't that be a crazy thing, like visiting somebody, the door opened and the Negro was in the doorway, filling it, standing there in pants and boots but without a shirt in that hot place and holding a long-barreled Walker that was already cocked.

They stood ten feet apart looking at each other, close enough so that no one could fire from the slope.

"I can kill you first," the Negro said, "if you raise that."

With his free hand, the left one, Bob Valdez motioned back over his shoulder. "There's a man there said you killed somebody a year ago."

"What man?"

"Said his name is Tanner."

The Negro shook his head, once each way.

"Said your name is Johnson."

"You know my name."

"I'm telling you what he said."

"Where'd I kill this man?"

"Huachuca."

The Negro hesitated. "That was some time ago I was in the Tenth. More than a year."

"You a deserter?"

"I served it out."

"Then you got something that says so."

"In the wagon, there's a bag there my things are in."

"Will you talk to this man Tanner?"

"If I can hold from hitting him one."

"Listen, why did you run this morning?"

"They come chasing. I don't know what they want." He lowered the gun a little, his brown-stained-looking tired eyes staring intently at Bob Valdez. "What would you do? They came on the run. Next thing I know they a-firing at us. So I pop in this place."

"Will you come with me and talk to him?"

The Negro hesitated again. Then shook his head. "I don't know him."

"Then he won't know you, uh?"

"He didn't know me this morning."

"All right," Bob Valdez said. "I'll get your paper says you were discharged. Then we'll show it to this man, uh?"

The Negro thought it over before he nodded, very slowly, as if still thinking. "All right. Bring him here, I'll say a few words to him."

Bob Valdez smiled a little. "You can point that gun some other way."

"Well . . ." the Negro said, "if everybody's friends." He lowered the Walker to his side.

The wagon was in the willow trees by the creek. Off to the right. But Bob Valdez did not turn right away in that direction. He backed away, watching Orlando Rincon for no reason that he knew of. Maybe because the man was holding a gun and that was reason enough.

He had backed off six or seven feet when Orlando Rincon shoved the Walker down into his belt. Bob Valdez turned and started for the trees.

This was when he looked across the pasture. He saw Mr. Tanner and R. L. Davis at the edge of the scrub trees but wasn't sure it was them. Something tried to tell him it was them, but he did not accept it until he was off to the right, out of the line of fire, and by then the time to yell at them or run toward them was past, for R. L. Davis had the Winchester up and was firing.

They say R. L. Davis was drunk or he would have pinned him square. As it was the bullet shaved Rincon and plowed past him into the hut.

Bob Valdez saw him half turn, either to go inside or look inside, and as he came around again saw the man's eyes on him and his hand pulling the Walker from his belt.

"They weren't supposed to," Bob Valdez said, holding one hand out as if to stop Rincon. "Listen, they weren't supposed to do that!"

The Walker was out of Rincon's belt and he was cocking it. "Don't!" Bob Valdez yelled. "Don't!" Looking right in the man's eyes and seeing it was no use and suddenly hurrying, jerking the shotgun up and pulling both triggers so that the explosions came out in one big blast and Orlando Rincon was spun and thrown back inside.

They came out across the pasture to have a look at the carcass, some going inside where they found the woman also dead, killed by a rifle bullet. They noticed she would have had a child in a few months. Those by the doorway made room as Mr. Tanner and R. L. Davis approached.

Diego Luz came over by Bob Valdez, who had not moved. Valdez stood watching them and he saw Mr. Tanner look down at Rincon and after a moment shake his head.

"It looked like him," Mr. Tanner said. "It sure looked like him."

He saw R. L. Davis squint at Mr. Tanner. "It ain't the one you said?"

Mr. Tanner shook his head again. "I've seen him before, though. Know I've seen him somewheres."

Valdez saw R. L. Davis shrug. "You ask me, they all look alike." He was yawning then, fooling with his hat, and then his eyes swiveled over at Bob Valdez standing with the empty shotgun.

"Constable," R. L. Davis said, "you went and killed the wrong coon."

Bob Valdez started for him, raising the shotgun to swing it like a club, but Diego Luz drew his revolver and came down with it and Valdez dropped to the ground.

Some three years later there was a piece in the paper about a Robert Eladio Valdez who had been hanged for murder in Tularosa, New Mexico. He had shot a man coming out of the Regent Hotel, called him an unprintable name, and shot him four times. This Valdez had previously killed a man in Contention and two in Sands during a bank holdup, had been caught once, escaped from the jail in Mesilla before trial, and identified another time during a holdup near Lordsburg.

"If it is the same Bob Valdez used to live here," Mr. Beaudry said, "it's good we got rid of him."

"Well, it could be," Mr. Malsom said. "But I guess there are Bob Valdezes all over."

"You wonder what gets into them," Mr. Beaudry said.

The stories contained in this volume originally appeared in the following publications:

"Trail of the Apache," *Argosy*, December 1951

"You Never See Apaches . . . ," *Dime Western Magazine*, September 1952

"The Colonel's Lady," *Zane Grey's Western*, November 1952

"The Rustlers," *Zane Grey's Western*, February 1953

"The Big Hunt," *Western Magazine*, April 1953

"The Boy Who Smiled," *Gunsmoke*, June 1953

"Only Good Ones," *Western Roundup*, New York, Macmillan, 1961 (*Western Writers of America Anthology*)